The
Idea
of You

J. Desails

Printed in the United States of America
First Printing, 2017

For J.
Thank you for always loving me.
Amor Vincit Omnia

Chapter One

    I woke up feeling restless in a fog, but completely at peace. My mind was at ease, this was my favorite place to be, right before the chaos of my life awakened me, the same as when you put your foot in to test the water, and someone pushes you into the deep end. I stretched out my arms, glanced toward the sun beaming in my window, and heard the loud obnoxious snore of my best friend, Jane. I closed my eyes hoping for just ten more minutes of sleep; simultaneously my alarm went off. Jane jumped up "what are you making for breakfast?" *Seriously,* I thought. She is living in my apartment, rent-free and wants a chef and maid well, not today. Honestly not most mornings either.

    "Jane, you've got to handle this one on your own I have clients this morning remember, it's not always about you." Even though we both know it is always about her. I don't know of a single person that hasn't fallen for her instant charm, and she often uses it to her advantage; hence her living here with me.

    Jane grew up in the suburbs, just an hour away from the city. She was far enough away to stay out of trouble, but too close to resist it. She had long dark hair, which matched her olive skin, all of which was highlighted by her ice blue eyes. Her voice was inviting and friendly, yet demanding simultaneously. I have yet to meet a man to refuse to buy her a drink upon her request, and a woman who doesn't envy her powers.

    Jane and I met in our early twenties, seeking fresh starts in New York City. She has been my full-time unlicensed therapist, alibi, and often my comedic relief for seven years. As much as I have fallen in love with the city, I have fallen in love with her.

    "Bells do you want me to walk with you to the office?" She had nothing better to do than to follow me, this was the consistency of our friendship, she was my shadow and I was her ray of sunshine.

"Sure, but you're buying me coffee." I mumbled. "Absolutely, which one of your cards should I use?" She quickly spat.

I laugh every time I hear Jane joke about using my money to buy me things. The fact is, fortunately about a year ago I got a big photography break, one of my satisfied clients was cousins with an A list celebrity who thought she would try using an amateur for her new fragrance. Turns out, I was better than I thought and once I aced that job, my name spread like wildfire.

Jane is still stuck back and forth between any job she can hold for more than two weeks, trouble is she spends more time getting the job then she does at actually working there. But I have to hand it to her; she somehow still "affords" to go out almost every night, mostly due to the fact I have never actually witnessed her paying for one of her own drinks.

I threw on a white blouse, tossed my hair up in a messy bun and grabbed my favorite dark denim jeans. I grabbed my bag, and apple and dashed out the door. My studio was five blocks from my new apartment, right in Manhattan. Who would have guessed? Not me that's for sure.

The one thing Jane had that I knew I would never possess was her confidence, sure I could change my hair color, diet and exercise, or get colored contacts, but I could never be as confident as her. "Bells, I'll just meet you at the office you're going way too fast this morning." I have always been a morning person, Jane however cannot comprehend why people wake up before twelve noon.

"That's fine, it would be the first time you were ever on time anyway."
"Blah blah blah," I see her flick me off in the reflection of my oversized sunglasses.

I always enjoyed my morning walks to work; they were often quiet even with the sounds of the city encompassing me. I could concentrate; plan my day and how each shot should lay out in my mind. Today I have a very important client, Ellen's dog. The animals are a big deal this day, and they are often my hardest clients. No matter what I do, they have the upper hand, and I have to work excessively to achieve the greatness that is expected of me even if expectations are seemingly impossible.

The thing about photography is, no matter how I envision my work; it must also grasp the vision of my client. Every client comes onto the set with a picture; I need to figure out what it is and how I get it. Ninety percent of my job is reading my client, developing a relationship with them and satisfying all of their needs. Basically, a high end call girl of photography.

My love for photography developed when I was a small child. A picture was all I had of my grandmother, and without that single photo, I would have nothing. There is only one visual aid that documents a woman who accomplished more than I could dream of. She raised six children, each to be beautiful people, and on top of all of this kept one man happy for forty-five years. I can't even convince my boyfriend of five years of being monogamous.

Once I could get my hands on a camera, and actually figure out how to work it I began taking photos of everything. Statistically speaking a love story like my grandparents is extinct, and I almost felt like I would try to capture what they had in every wedding, engagement or even print ad. My entire childhood was documented through my photos. My poor grandchildren will be bored out of their minds, wondering exactly how many albums they have to look at before the pain ends. *Ha*. Imagine, me having grandkids, what a joke.

I used to dream about having the perfect family; two kids, a dog and a white picket fence. This was before I fell into the city, and then the years slipped out of my hands like sand falling in-between the cracks. Now I am twenty-seven, currently living with my best friend, and having an occasional "sleepover" at my boyfriends, I never actually stay until the alarm goes off. I am without a doubt a perpetual seventeen-year-old.

Finally, at work, and greeted by Ellen's dog with a big wet nose in-between my crotch. *Fantastic*, without looking up I am sure that everyone is staring at me. "Whoshabooba" I heard her annoying voice, my assistant Becca.

Here we go, I think to myself, and maybe even out loud. Becca is a fantastically organized, overly excitable and ambitious assistant. That being said, she is also extremely irritating.

"Miss Izabella, the dog is here and ready." *Really?* As if she didn't see the dog in my crotch already. She is also the only person, other than my mother to call me by my full first name.

It took two hours of exhausting work, about a thousand photos that I would have to view and edit tonight, oh and finally, Jane showed up. At least she showed up with my coffee when I needed it. I got Becca to wrap up all of the equipment and finish with Ellen, and quietly I snuck out.

"Ugh I can't do the dogs anymore." I roll my eyes and look over at Jane, who delivers some fantastic news.

"Bo wants to pick you up in an hour for an afternoon date, told him I'd deliver the message." She smiled smitten. She knew that it was nearly impossible for Bo to be romantic, and for sure she would try to take partial credit.

Great I look like shit, the only day my boyfriend actually wants to pay attention to me. "Fine but you have to help me get ready." I figured I would meet him at his place, since he rarely took the time to walk to mine. I swear if I didn't put any effort into the relationship, there wouldn't be one.

Jane stayed at the studio and used all of the hair products and makeup that was out of the budget for both of us to use on a daily basis, part of the perks of owning my own studio. She curled my hair into big loose waves, and made me feel like I was a celebrity. I had always pushed her to pursue her love for cosmetology, but she always shut me down, most recently saying she was too old.

Bo and I have been "dating" for five years, monogamous for only two, although probably not completely monogamous either, let's call it *mainly monogamous*. Although that's a long time to spend with someone we have never taken our relationship beyond booty calls and cocktails. In fact, I can't even remember ever-discussing kids, marriage or moving in together. My relationship status is by no means ideal, but most days I am content with where I am.

An hour later I am knocking on his door, giving myself a pat on the back for looking so put together. Jane was my fairy Godmother···bippity boppity···..boo.

The second he answers the door, I am sure of the reason that I have stayed in this dead-end relationship. *He is beautiful.* He runs his hands nervously through his dark wavy hair and lets a glimpse of his perfect smile break through. I looked into his blue eyes as if I have never seen them before; it reminded me of how vampires compelled their victims. I let myself in without an invitation.

He placed his hand on the small of my back as I walked through the threshold. "Bells I want to take you somewhere special this afternoon don't get too comfortable." I wasn't certain of the emotion he was producing, which made me feel like the butterflies in my stomach could turn to bees at a moment's notice.

"'I'm just going to go freshen up quickly." I nonchalantly waved as I walked past him. His apartment is the exact definition of a bachelor pad. He has video games, a big screen television, an oversized bed that is constantly unmade, and nothing but cereal in the cupboards. You would never guess that he is a thirty-two-year-old and a very successful stockbroker, and that is why I began to fall for him.

I am always giving myself a reason to check out his apartment, I guess I am waiting to find the jewelry of another woman, or maybe the other woman herself, so I have a reason to leave. I never find anything, and I never leave.

Bo is sweet, he is charming and he is so much fun. He would be the most perfect escort to events, kind of like The Wedding Date, and ironically, he reminded me of a young Dermot Mulroney.

He also does not like commitment, and does not talk about his past. All of the above are fine by me, but sometimes I can't help but wonder. Even though I hate to admit it, because I revel in the fact that I have a causal relationship with him, I'm pretty sure I would be torn apart if I ever did find anything.

"Are you done scoping the place out yet?" He looks at me with a slight smirk. He's onto me. "Yeah, yeah, yeah let's go." Before I leave I take one last glance at the picture on his nightstand, of him and a beautiful woman, the picture tells a story. I've made up a different one every time that I see it, since Bo never tells me the true one. All that I get from him is that it was a good friend from the past, a story that I don't believe, and I can tell he doesn't either.

Our dates typically consist of brief coffee meetings, or fancy dinners followed by fantastic sex and me taking a cab home at 3am. So, meeting in the afternoon is out of the ordinary for both of us, especially since he is aware that I have already had coffee today.

"We are going to have a picnic in central park today, I thought the weather was nice, plus I missed you." Ok this is definitely weird. He placed his hand on the small of my back and we began the fifteen-minute walk. I keep thinking to myself, this is it; he is finally breaking up with me.

We finally get to the park, he grabs us sandwiches from the deli and we sit on the steps in front of the fountain. I could sit here and people watch all day. I make up stories about half of them in my head, lavish love stories mostly. I often wonder how many of them are the fake kind of Facebook types, you know the ones, #MCM every single Monday, but realistically cannot stand each other. I never got the point of it, why is it so important to portray something so publicly that your fourth-grade teacher can like the picture of you and the guy you've been sleeping with for years, praying you'll eventually get a ring. If he hasn't put a ring on your finger within the first three years, there's probably a reason. I hear Bo let out a soft sigh and my butterflies are now bees.

"Bells, you know I care deeply for you." Here we go. I braced myself for the inevitable. My fingers gripped the edge of the bench, readying my body for the push off and sprint I was about to take. I always run, never face my problems, I guess that's my biggest problem.

"I can't see us together forever, but I can't see us apart either. Where do we stand?"

He was nervously running his fingers through his hair. I could see a small trace of sweat on his forehead and his breathing was definitely labored.

Great fucking question Bo, way to waste five years of my life! Why do we do this, us women, we are completely ok with the way things are, even if we seem to be content until they get changed and then we get pissed. I felt like the women who post the #MCM, waiting for the ring, knowing it probably won't ever come, at least not from this guy.

"I don't know Bo you tell me, it seems it's your world and I'm just along for the ride."

"I was thinking we should move in together, twice a week." My jaw drops and I am sure he sees it. So, then I let him have it. If he wanted to twist the knife in my stomach he had succeeded.

"What the hell is that supposed to mean twice a week? You either do it or you don't asshole. I can't waste any more time in this relationship, you said it yourself you can't see us together forever so why waste any more time, I am done."

I threw my sandwich down and didn't remember anything in between that conversation and me arriving at my front door. Hunched over trying to catch my breath I realized I had done it once again, I ran. Part of me didn't want to walk in and deal with Jane's questions; the other part of me knew I needed her. I opened the door, and she glanced in my direction stood up and ran towards me. For the first time Jane didn't say a word she just hugged me and that's all I needed.

Chapter Two

"Fuck him, he's a prick." My heart sank, knowing that those words aren't even close to being true. We sat on the couch eating vanilla bean ice cream and immediately regretting each bite.

"Oh yeah you got another one of those red envelopes in the mail today."
My heart rate increased momentarily, as I knew this would give me a few moments of relief. I picked up the envelope and ripped it open, normally I was a little more careful.

Iz,
        How are you girl? I miss you so much.
Sorry I can't write much this time, busy as always but I'll see you in a few weeks for the graduation, right?
Love ya,
Jer

Jeremy. Seeing his handwriting made me remember that I am not alone in anything. I talk to Jer four times a week at least, but he still manages to write me a letter once a week and I do the same. When I moved here we both complained about how all we ever get in the mail is bills, and it was so depressing checking the mailbox. Jer wanted to give me a reason to be excited. He always sent his in a red envelope, and I sent him mine in blue.

He reminded me about the graduation, our little brothers are graduating from high school together. It will be a weekend full of fun, including all the questions I will get like why I am not married and pregnant yet, and who my #MCM is currently. For the small town that I am from I am about seven years late on starting a family. My mother will be happy to see me, and I can't wait to eat all the fattening shit she cooks. For one weekend I can be the old Izzie, forget about all work that I need to get done and relax.

"Bells, sorry to bother you but Bo is at the door." *Shit.* I don't want to deal with this issue at all. I'd like to pretend it would just dissolve on its own, that he would go down without a fight, but I knew that we both had to have the last word. Before I could get up to meet him at the door I heard his deep voice, and it sent chills down my spine.

"B, we need to talk. Alone." He gave Jane a glance and she shot one right over at me. "It's fine Jane." She quickly grabbed her purse and darted, I didn't blame her.

I calmly sat down on my bed and he came over and put his hand on my face. I immediately felt his hand wet with my tears. I don't know why I was crying, I ended it, but for some reason I couldn't hold them back anymore.

"B, please let me first apologize. The reason that I wanted you to live with me two days a week was because I didn't want to overwhelm you, not because I can't handle you for more." I couldn't tell if this was passive aggressive Bo, charming Bo, or genuine Bo.

"I want to take things to the next level because if we don't do it now, we never will." He was being honest and open. Something I knew existed in him, but rarely witnessed.

He was right about that, I always assumed we never would be more than what we always were. I played the scenario in my head, over and over again and I thought, *why not?* Jane could stay here, so if I needed to I could come back, although I will have to make her pay rent, oh and she can't have sex with anyone in my bed. Slowly I took a deep breath in and exhaled the word··· "Yes."

I feel like I just committed myself to marriage. I felt overwhelmed with emotion and thought maybe he was right, we should take it two days a week, but that would make me a hypocrite. Maybe we should have discussed it more, but I also love to run from confrontation oh, and also all of my emotions.

"I'll have your things packed for you and taken to my place while you're home for the graduations." *I'd be an idiot not to love him.* I slowly leaned in and kissed him and more tears streamed down my face except this time they were happy ones.

In one swift motion he pulled me onto his lap, I stared into his eyes because quite honestly it was hard not to. His kiss always starts gentle, like a first kiss date and always ends like I am his and only his and he wants to make sure everyone in the world knows it.

I felt his hand creep up my back and unsnap my bra; the buttons from my shirt slowly began unbuttoning themselves and with one arm behind me, lays me softly on my back. I felt the passion from his kiss travel down my neck making it almost impossible to not let out a whimper of pleasure. When I felt him spread my legs open, the butterflies were back. I looked up and realized I was making love to one of the most beautiful men I have ever laid my eyes on. This time was different, this time I was emotional. The sex was always great, amazing actually, but this time was the first time I felt like we were actually in a relationship. This was the first time while he was inside of me that I told him I loved him.

Chapter Three

When Jane comes home to our apartment
with me by myself, she thinks the worst. Her eyes
are so big and her mouth is wide open, I can see
the disbelief written on her face.

"I'm moving in with him."

"No fucking way." Her honesty never
ceases for anyone. Whereas I like to hide my
emotions, she loves to embellish hers and take
them up to level ten···always.

"I mean, I've only been gone for two fucking
hours, how is it even possible you've decided to
move in with Mcdreamy, I'm sure you also had
amazing makeup sex and all I did was get a latte!"

"Well I think this is overdue, I mean why
shouldn't I move in with him?"

"Um, because who will take care of me?"

"Ah, Jane I think it's time for you to grow up
and move off of my couch into my bed."

"Really? You trust me that much?" As she
rolls her eyes and throws her empty latte cup at
me.

"You do know that there is a phone number
on your cup, right?"

"Yeah, but he is a barrister, girl I need big
money. Do you have any idea how stupid these
women are marrying for love?"

The sarcastic tone in her voice is
unrecognizable. My poor Jane wanted more than
anything to fall in love, but she thinks it's not in the
cards for her, so her next mission: marry for
money.

"Can I redecorate in here?" I could tell she
was holding that in for all of thirty seconds.

"Really Jane? It's smaller than your closet at
your parents' house, there isn't much you can do,
but sure." She looked at me quite serious "if you
need to come home, don't hesitate." I laughed, "I

know bitch, I still own this place!" Suddenly I remembered there was something else I had to do, I had to tell Jer.

"I'll definitely tell him at the graduation." I said out loud to myself in front of my mirror. That way he won't think I am as crazy as I really am since I have been bitching to him about Bo for the past two years. That's the catch twenty-two with your best friend, you tell them all your relationship secrets, what you really want and if they are truly looking out for your best interest they will be the first to judge you when you do something incredibly stupid. I think moving in with Bo puts me at the top of that list.

"Bells, George called and needs you to do a quick shoot for one of his new clients. Could you do it in an hour?" I jumped at the door slamming as I heard Becca's voice behind me. I glance over my shoulder trying to figure out how Becca broke into my apartment. I looked over at Jane who shrugged her shoulders and walked out the door. I'm sure she was headed to Neiman Marcus with my credit card to redecorate my apartment.

"I guess so Becca, since I am guessing you already told him yes." She glared at me, both of us knowing its true. She could sense the anger in my voice, but also knew me well enough to know that I cannot hold a grudge.

I threw on a bra, loose tank top and some jean shorts. Lightly added some makeup since all of George's clients are models, and ran out the door.

I always did George's photo shoots at his apartment; he had a huge room with a drape already set up for me. These last-minute calls were frequent, especially when he is promising new clients stardom and trying to sign them faster than any of the other thousands of agents in NYC.

I ran up the steps and knocked on George's door, pondering where I would be without him. Probably still working 9-5 in the art gallery, selling portraits that were worth more than my parent's home.

George was a frequent purchaser for those exact art pieces. We got along great from the start, after about five months of working there he caught a glimpse of my photos that I was editing on my desk. I remember the conversation like it was yesterday.

"Bells, my dear why is it that you don't hang these beautiful photos in here? I'd pay just as much to have them as the last twelve."

My first thought was that he was just being kind. After I saw the seriousness in his eyes, I was overcome with shock. My mouth dropped, he was the first person to acknowledge that I could actually do this; I could actually be successful as a photographer. The conversation was short and sweet, after that moment George started using me to shoot all of his new clients. Then when they got bigger, they took me with them. Thus, I owe George for all of my success.

With a quick movement the door flew open, and George's arms were around me. He was like a father to me, my New York Guru. Many a times he was also my designated driver, and hangover healer. "It's always so fantastic to see you Bells, listen this one is great, but he's a country boy so take it easy on him." Although I've heard this a hundred times, I felt his passion about this one.

I threw up my long blond hair into a big messy bun, and started working on the camera. I remembered when I first moved here, I had mousy brown hair, a terrible closet and a bad country accent. I laughed quietly to myself wondering if this "country boy" would even be able to tell that I was also from the country. It seems that though George is aware, he never seems to actually acknowledge where I am from. It makes me proud that I fit in as a New Yorker, I've worked my ass off to mask my accent and hide my true identity. Finally, I was all set to go when I slowly turned around and heard his voice⋯

"Holy Shit."

George and I both stared in complete silence. Then George said something to break the ice.

"She's cute, but she isn't that cute." Laughing nervously.

"Bella." The words were a whisper, almost in confusion.

"Todd, good to see you." My mind went completely blank, and filled with high school memories.

I hated school parties, but Jer told me I had to go to this one. "It'll be different." He promised. I hated parties because for one, I was always the odd one out. I never quite fit into a crowd, not that I was an outcast, just more so in-between all of the crowds. Everyone at parties however, picked their group and stuck to it. Todd was that boy, the star Quarterback and Homecoming King every single year. He was Chapel Run's very own cliché.

I have loved Todd since I was in sixth grade; he was the first boy I ever liked, and the last until I moved to New York. He was also the boy I knew I could never have.

It wasn't until that party that Jer made me go to that I even realized he knew who I was. I was pissed at Jer, for leaving me to talk to a new girl, who was a friend of a friend so I decided to go home early. I came out to my car and saw that my tires had been slashed, yet another reason that I never went to those lame ass parties. Frustrated because I had no cell phone at the time, I sat on the hood of my car and sobbed. It was one of those moments you look back on and realize that you were being completely absurd but, in the moment,, you had no control.

After five minutes of feeling sorry for myself crying, I felt a hand on my shoulder. I shoved it off before it could even find its placement.

"Get the fuck off of me Jer."

"Um, Bella? Are you ok? Did Jer do something to you?"

I froze, half embarrassed and half shocked that Todd was speaking to me, and I looked like a complete fool.

"Yes, sorry. Someone just slashed my tires, and I was nervous I wouldn't be able to find a way home for a while." That sounded stupid. I was visibly shaking as he held out his hand to help me off the car. It was the awkward shake, where you try to hide the fact that you're shaking.

"I'm heading out too, can I drop you home?" I gazed at him confused, knowing that he had only just arrived to the party.

"That would be great actually, thanks." I grabbed my purse, and drove home with the only boy I ever loved, and he had no idea.

The conversation on the way home was expected. Barely any words were spoken, since we really had nothing in common. I was thankful I didn't live far, yet simultaneously disappointed. Before I knew it, he was walking my up to the front porch.

I turned quickly to thank him, and he placed his lips softly on mine. I closed my eyes and kissed him back as if we had been dating for years. He pulled away, and softly said "Goodnight," and turned to leave. I felt the tears in my eyes start to pool. *What the fuck just happened?* He walked away so casually, like nothing even happened and I started to wonder if maybe I had dreamt that part up.

"Too bad we graduate in a week, I would have loved to see where this thing would have gone." And that was it. Those were the last words I heard from Todd, ten years ago.

Back to reality, "Bells, you know this guy?" George asked in excitement, hoping it would help him seal the deal.

"Yeah, you could say that." I smiled softly and started to take my pictures.
I was at a loss for words, and Todd kept trying to talk in-between photos but I kept telling him that I needed him to be quiet until the end of the shoot. Honestly, I needed to buy time; I had no idea what to say to him. Should I tell him that he looks ten times better than the last time that I saw him, that he broke my heart and never knew it, or that I still thought about him all the time? What the hell was I going to do?

George glanced over at me, and I knew that he could tell I was prolonging the shoot. I needed more time to think. When I was taking the pictures, it was like I was on a treadmill, in the zone. I no longer had to put my full concentration on headshots, it was so monotonous I could do it half asleep, or hung over. So, I took advantage and mentally checked out of my job. Finally, after an hour and a half, I nodded, informing George that I had enough shots.

"No shit." George huffed under his breath. He was scrolling through his phone probably searching for the next starlet if Todd didn't work out.

I turned away packing up my camera, when I felt his hand on my shoulder. I immediately got goose bumps, it was the same feeling I had on my shoulder ten years ago and it felt as if he had touched a painful scar, the ones you've had so long they are forgotten, until someone brings them to your attention again.

Maybe I was being melodramatic about what happened back then, but the fact is he knew he fucked with my head. How could you possibly kiss someone, say that and leave?

"Bella, how have you been? It's been years, I would have never recognized you if it wasn't for that smile."

Ugh don't start with me Todd, I was letting my anger show.

"I've been wonderful, thanks for asking." I politely smiled.

"That's it? Really? Ten years and that's all I get?"

He was inviting himself into my world, and I was going to fight against it. *Was I the only one that remembered vividly what he did?*

"I guess so. I'm quite busy these days." I had a pang of excitement knowing that I was established in the big city and he was still trying to do something with his life. Then immediately following that excitement, I felt disappointment in myself for feeling that way. Damn conscience.

"Bella, can I at least take you out for a drink?"
Here we go⋯

Chapter Four

"Todd, I have to run back to my apartment to drop my camera off and get changed. If you want to come with me I can drive us somewhere after to get drinks."

"Absolutely. Love to." He smiled and I was again conscious of my heartbeat.

He helped me pack up my things, and followed me like a puppy all the way home. *How Ironic.* I remember being in his shoes for my entire high school career, just not as obvious. My eyes glanced over my shoulder as I took him in. He is everything I remembered and better. His defined jaw line, naturally golden highlighted hair, and beautifully chiseled abs (I had to look, I was taking pictures.) I took in a deep breath, that almost hurt. How will I explain to Bo that I am going out with this gorgeous man, who might I add Bo does know that I had a crush on throughout high school. Fortunately, he is completely unaware, as is every other person on this earth about our first and last kiss.

"You really have changed Bella, wow." I bat my lashes and blushed.

"Todd, it would be a miracle if you lasted three months in NYC without changing, I guess you could say I just evolved."

"I mean it Bella, you look amazing."

I felt him place his hand on my lower back, and it felt right so I didn't try to move him.

I got butterflies in my stomach, that's a first for me, since the first kiss that we shared in high school. Bo never gave me butterflies, maybe because I always thought we would never last. He was great, but not a great love. Not the kind of guy you write stories about great. I had written the story of Todd and I thousands of times in my head, each one slightly different than the last, all of them end up with us married with five kids. And here he is.

"Well this is my place; do you want to hang out down here or would you like to come up while I get ready?" I paused for a second, wondering if I shouldn't have asked him to come up.

"I'll come up." *Of course, you will.*

I heard Jane talking to someone before I could open the door, as I placed my key in the hole, I felt her tug on the other side. "Ghetto apartment" I heard her muffle.

She opened and stared past me, obviously looking at Todd; he is exactly her type. "Er···Jane this is Todd." I said quickly hoping to avoid the next twenty-five questions.

"Hi Todd." She leaned over and whispered into my ear "Nice, are you trying to make Bo jealous?"

"Of course not. Todd is an old friend." Then my body froze as I saw Bo step out behind Jane.

"Todd. Bo, Bella's boyfriend." Oh, now after five years he wants to claim me. I nervously started explaining the situation, trying to read the expression on Bo's face.

"It's a long story, so here's the short version, Todd is in town, he is Georges model of the moment, and I did his shoot. Small city huh? Anyway, we are going to grab a drink and I'll be back in a little bit." Bo looked at me realizing what I was trying to do, rush out and avoid confrontation. I hate confrontation.

"Sure doll, I brought by some boxes for your belongings. I'll see you tomorrow." Then he leaned over and kissed me on the cheek and softly whispered "Don't think I don't fucking remember who this guy is."

Really? I rolled my eyes and jabbed him in the side slightly with my elbow. I will deal with him tomorrow. *Asshole.* Well I was going to change into jeans and a shirt but now Bo has pissed me off, so it's my heels and short dress! I got ready quickly as possible, Jane was shooting the shit with Todd, probably asking him for his number by now. I glanced at myself in the mirror and was satisfied. I had long loose curls from my sock bun earlier, red lipstick, red heels, black dress and loads of mascara. I looked borderline slutty, Bo would be pissed and I fucking loved it.

"You ready Todd?" I said in my sexy voice. I'm sure I sounded ridiculous.

"Wow. Bella, what happened to you?" His eyes were glued to me.

I was feeling that funniness in my stomach again and nervously smiled. I took a deep breath and walked out of my apartment with my arm interlocked in Todd's.

Of course, when I walked out of the building Bo was still there, across the street. *Real fucking sneaky, dumbass.* I saw him take one look at us and then look away in disgust. Part of me felt bad for him, because I did care about him, and we did just decide to move in together, but how dare he bring up parts of my past that I told him, as if they would affect my future. Although by doing that, he may have just changed our destiny.

Chapter Five

"So, Bella, what is this about you being some hot shot photographer?"

"er···I ugh well I'm not that big of a deal." I hoped he would believe that, but we both knew better. My mom brags about me all the time, even though she has no idea what my life is like.

"Yeah well George seemed to think otherwise, he was telling me all about you before you came. Ironic how I already knew more about you than he did."

"Really, because the last time we spoke you said you wish you knew me better." Shit. I really just said that.

"Oh, um, yeah, well sorry. Where are we going?" He stared at the ground.

Just like that, subject changed and our night went on. We ended up having a few drinks, laughed about old high school classmates, but rarely talked about ourselves. I did manage to get out of him that he got into modeling because his father's auto shop just "wasn't his thing." I thought it was hilarious how modeling was; I mean I always felt funny about guys who pursued it on their own without being discovered. Then I realized I might not have the whole story anyway, since really George could have just stumbled across him.

"Well listen it's been great but I have some errands to run pretty early tomorrow, so I'll take you back to your hotel."

I really didn't have to run errands, but the truth is the night had gone well, I figured I might as well end it well now before I find a way to screw it up.

"Yeah, definitely. I appreciate the ride and tonight was great. Good catching up with you." We drove back to his hotel, and I began thinking about how excited I was to call Jer and tell him. He wouldn't believe it, and he would be just as surprised as I was. I decided I needed to wait for the conversation I was going to have with Bo. I don't have the energy right now, and I sure as hell don't feel like coming off my Todd high yet.

As we pulled up to the hotel, he went in for an awkward still in our seats, car hug. The next thing I know we are in a full out passionate make out session. I felt his hand on my jaw, his tongue slowly and gently entering my mouth, I tried to make my body resist, and it fought me the whole way. It felt like hours had gone by when the kiss ended, and then he stared at me. Neither of us knew what to say, or wanted to say anything for that matter. I felt the word vomit coming up, just as I was about to open my mouth and tell him to fuck off, for doing this to me again, he opened his.

"Bella, I know I didn't have the right to do that. Christ, I just met your boyfriend three hours ago. I don't know what your situation is, and I know you don't know mine but the truth is, I always wanted to get to know you better. I just didn't think that you would want to get to know me." I'm calling it..BULLSHIT! Todd could have any girl and he knew it.

"Todd, it's late, you've been drinking. Here is my number call me anytime, but tonight this conversation is not happening." I was amazing myself these days. Ten years ago, I wanted to tell him I loved him the second his lips touched mine, and now I am telling him to call me some other time. I have some serious issues, and think that maybe I should see a therapist···. or I could just talk to Jane and Jer.

The whole drive home, I played my music super loud and pretended as if I was seventeen again. No Bo, Todd didn't notice me, and Jer and I were taking on the world. Ha. I needed to call him, I needed to vent to him.

Four rings and right to voicemail. Well that sucks. Jane I could talk to, but she wouldn't understand the situation in the same light that Jer would. But I knew if I told him about tonight, all of tonight that I would also have to tell him about the night after the party in high school. Jer and I didn't have secrets, except that one. I didn't want to tell him at the time because he would have confronted Todd, and embarrassed me, most likely in front of the entire school.

Jer was a sweetheart, but had a reputation for being a badass. I guess he was only a sweetheart to me, and whatever girl he was dating at the moment. I felt my phones vibrations, and looked down at the screen *Jer Bear,* giggling because I still don't think he has any idea he is in my phone under that name. I picked up without even thinking about what I was going to say, it's a bad habit I couldn't break if he called me I had to answer.

"Iz, what's up?" He sounded out of breath.

"Oh, nothing just wanted to hear your voice." He could tell I was lying.

"Oh. That's weird." He said in his sarcastic voice.

"Yeah, well now that I have I guess I can hang up."

"Don't be such a loser Iz. Are you excited about next week?"

"Yeah, can't wait. How are our little broski's? Are they excited to be done with school?" I suddenly realized it has been two months since my brother and I have spoken, and though what we have is far from a healthy relationship, I missed him.

"Yeah you could say that. I'm really excited to see you Iz, and I've met a girl I want you to meet, she is⋯" there was a long pause.

"AMAZING." *What the fuck*, I felt like the air in my lungs was kicked out of me.

"Really? Wow Jer that's great. You know that's the word, right?? Our code word, you just used it!" Years ago, Jer told me that amazing was the best compliment you could give anyone, and he only ever used it referring to me. I guess I knew at some point in time I would have to grow up and here it about someone else too. I just thought when I heard it I would be happy for him, not jealous.

"Yeah, I know Iz and I didn't want to tell you over the phone but I couldn't wait. I think she may be the one."

"Pump the brakes Jer. How long have you been with her? I mean it couldn't have been long enough to talk about marriage, I talked to you two days ago."

"I've known her for about a month. She comes into the pub, and well finally we went on a date two nights ago and I can't stop thinking about her."

Two fucking nights? That's it. I'll be looking this girl up on the Internet that's for sure. I knew that Jer could win the girls hearts, being the heartthrob bar owner and everything.

"That's great Jer, so happy for you can't wait to meet her."

"Well anything new with you?" I froze.

"Nope. Nothing new." I just lied to my best friend, first about moving in with Bo and next about just kissing Todd. I knew if I told him he would be in the city before dawn ready to beat the shit out of Todd, and I wasn't quite sure I wanted that to happen yet.

"Alright Iz, gotta go. See you next week. You bringing Jane?"

"Of course, I'm her light, and she is my annoying little mosquito. See ya Jer." I slammed the phone shut, not waiting for his response.

When Jer first met Jane, that's what he called her. And its kind of stuck···she is secretly in his phone under mosquito! I finally got home and threw myself into my bed. I looked over at all of the boxes Bo had brought me, I immediately felt guilty about the kiss I had just shared with Todd. Then it hit me, my wave of tears. I laced my pillow with hundreds of tears, and fell fast asleep.

The next morning, I woke up to Jane, in my face. I rolled right back over and started hoping that it would make her go away. Not likely···

"So, do you want to talk about what the hell happened last night?"

"Nothing. I don't know what you are talking about Jane."

"Hmmm. So, the pillows with the wet mascara all over them, that was nothing?"

I should have taken my makeup off, damnit since when is Jane a PI?

"I really am not ready to talk about it." I almost shouted.

"Well are you ready to talk about the 12 missed calls from Bo or Todd who is outside of our apartment right now?"

Fuck! I told him to call and now he is pissing me off. I look like shit I am sure, I can tell by the way Jane is staring at me.

"Tell him to wait down stairs I'll be down in ten."

"Really ten that's all you think you need? Clearly you haven't looked in the mirror."

"Just tell him ten damn it!"

I watched her roll her eyes, I'm sure that she is already running a thousand scenarios through her head right now. I climbed out of bed and went into the bathroom. She was right, I was a mess my face was covered in black mascara and my red lipstick was also smeared, maybe from the kiss or maybe from the pillow. I touched my lips softly remembering the kiss and how good it felt, and I momentarily felt forlorn, wondering how I could possibly tell Bo. I was pissed at him, but that gave me no right to kiss another man. But it wasn't just any man, it was the boy I had loved most of my life. And he was better than I remembered him. I'm all kinds of fucked up right now. But as I start to reapply fresh makeup and let my hair down, I realize that I am about to be a woman that I wouldn't be proud of.

Chapter Six

"Wow Bella, do you wake up looking like this?"

I felt my phone vibrating in my purse; I already know who it was so I ignored it. I have no idea what to say to Bo right now, do I admit that I kissed him? Do I even want to be with Bo? Ugh. I am so glad that in a week I will be home and I can forget all of this for a week. Maybe Jer can help me figure things out.

"No Todd, don't get excited, I only look like this when I am trying to impress someone." What the hell am I doing?

"Central park? I've never been and thought since it was nice we could go."

"Sure Todd, anything for you." I was clearly channeling seventeen-year-old Bella.

We walked forever, and I loved watching him swallow hard in amazement of the city. I remember feeling the same way when I first got here. You're overwhelmed, in awe and scared to death all at the same time. Kind of how I felt every time Todd would brush his hand against mine.

"Bella, look I don't know what the deal is with that guy, but I know you better than that. He isn't your type and I would really love to get to know you. I am only in town for three more days and then I am heading home to help my Dad until I get some callbacks. Can we try to see where this thing goes?"

If this were ten years ago the question would be rhetorical. Yes, I have been waiting for you to ask me for years, or no because finally my boyfriend of five years wants to commit to our relationship?

"Sure, but let's get one thing straight, this isn't a thing yet, and I am not sleeping with you." *What am I thinking?*

"Ah Bella, glad to see you haven't changed much." I sighed, because this sentence was moot since he really had no clue who I was in any aspect.

We finally reached Central Park and we sat in front of the famous fountain. I could stare at his beautiful face all day in amazement. He slowly put his hand on mine, and I allowed it surprising myself.

"What makes you so interested in me now all of a sudden? My success? I mean I just don't get it Todd you wanted nothing to do with me in high school."

"Well for one Bella, clearly you are no high schooler any more. You look divine, amazing even." I cringed thinking about Jer and how he used that word last night. I was still jealous.

" I just always thought you were a good person in high school, it's no surprise I was a man whore" he chuckles, "and I am so glad now that nothing ever happened to us then, because I finally get to be the man I want to be, with a girl I thought would never have me."

"Todd, I think you are twenty steps ahead of yourself. We are just friends. Old friends that are getting to know the new version of each other."

I couldn't help but think to myself that he had an ulterior motive. I glanced down at my phone and saw twenty missed calls from Bo. I used this to escape the awkward situation I found myself in, with the man of my dreams.

"Sorry Todd, I have to take this."

He looked disappointed, like he had so much he needed to say, but I wasn't ready to hear it yet.

"Hello? Bells you there? Did you really pick up?"

"Yes. What's up Bo?"

"Oh Bells, I am so sorry. Please don't be mad at me. We were just moving on, then I saw him, I thought you were getting scared off. Can you please meet me at my place for dinner tonight?"

"Of course, Bo."

Bo actually sounded worried that I would leave him. That's a first. I wonder why now, this all has to happen to me. Never in my life have two gorgeous men wanted me simultaneously, if even at all. I feel blessed and cursed all at the same time.

   I finished the afternoon with Todd in the park. He agreed to cool it off a little bit, but still wanted to spend all of our time together while he was in town. I agreed to eighty percent. As much as I wanted to give myself all to Todd, part of me held back knowing that there is something else going on. This situation is probably nothing more than a recipe for disaster. I was the eye of the hurricane, but one of my favorite things is dancing in the rain.

   When we walked back to my place, I made plans to meet Todd for lunch tomorrow. He would meet me here again and we would venture out into the concrete jungle together. I started to get knots in my stomach knowing that I would have to not only confess to my lunch with Todd this afternoon, but also tell Bo that I made plans with him for tomorrow. Here goes nothing.

Chapter Seven

I knocked softly on the door, and waited for what seemed like forever. Finally, Bo answered and looked even more perfect then I remembered. He smiled slightly, almost as an apology. I forgave him already, and hoped that he would be able to forgive me.

"Bells, come in." I looked around and my jaw dropped. There were candles everywhere, rose petals on the bed. Who is this man?

"Welcome home." My stomach felt sick. I wasn't sure that I was ready to commit to it anymore.

"I···I.. you did this all for me?"

"No Bells, the girl that's going to walk through the door right after you, of course this is for you." He was such a smart ass sometimes.

"I have no idea what to say." I stared at the bed, and glanced to the nightstand, the picture was gone.

"The good news is, you don't have to say anything."

Bo reached over to me and pulled me in close. I felt his hands on my lower back moving downward. Bo never touched me like this, it was always fast and right to the point. I could feel his emotions, and for Bo it was never about emotions. Taking his newly freed hand, he started to slowly unbutton my shirt. I have never wanted him more.

My shirt was completely open and worked his mouth from mine down to the top button of my jeans. *Thank God I am wearing super cute underwear.* Even though I've had him hundreds of times before this, somehow it felt like our first. The next hour and a half I were his only, and he was mine. After, I laid in his bed with his arms around me, another first for us.

"Bells, stay the night?" Of course, I didn't bring any clothes, assuming I would be hailing a cab at 3 am.

"If that's what you really want."

"What I really want, is you, all of you, over and over again."

In that moment, I wanted the same thing. Bo and I had each other, over and over again and for the first time in five years, I stayed until the morning.

I woke up to an empty bed, and wasn't surprised I am sure Bo had gone off to work. I rolled over and grabbed the comforters over my head, when I felt him jump on me.

"Ahhhh Bo, you scared the shit out of me!"

"Did you really think I would leave you without a kiss on our first sleepover?"

Is it even possible that I am falling for a man that I've already had hundreds of times before?

He was wearing his dress pants and his button-down shirt, which was carelessly, unbuttoned giving me a reminder of how perfect his body was. I placed my hand on his chest and then reached up behind his neck to pull him into me. Something was different about this Bo, he wanted me to stay here last night and I don't think that it even had anything to do with Todd. Something changed; maybe it was the picture that was no longer next to his bed. I don't know what did it, but I needed him to stay this way.

"Do you have to go to work?" I pouted my lips.

"Bells, you already know the answer or you wouldn't have asked."

I watched him leave, and sank back into this new reality, that I have fallen in love with a man that I have already had for five years. My thoughts were briefly interrupted by my cell phone ringing, I already knew who it was before I answered.

"Good morning Jane." I said, knowing the words about to come out of her mouth "I know Jane, yes I slept over, yes it was premeditated, and you're not going to believe this but I think I am in love with him."

"What the hell." She sounded out of breath.

"Taking the stairs again huh?" I laughed. "Shut up

you bitch, but yes I took the steps. I cannot believe this. You really think you love him?"
"Yes, I really do."
"Well fine, can we have lunch to discuss the details?" Oh shit. I had lunch plans with Todd, and Jane in this moment would not approve.
"I have to go see Todd, it will be the last time I see him before he leaves I promise." I could feel the judgment in her voice as she softly told me she would settle for dinner.

Even though Bo wasn't here, I didn't want to leave. I could still smell him, as if he was still here next to me. I closed my eyes tightly hoping he still was. I replayed last night over and over again in my head. Maybe we were meant for each other all along, I just had to wait for the right moment and now I was in it. I heard the doorknob turn, and immediately felt sick. I was waiting for her to walk in, I am sure this was a dream, and I was waiting to wake up. As I braced myself for another woman, his face appeared from behind the door.

"Fuck it, I called out sick. I need you, right now, and every hour after that." I could feel the smile on my lips as he pounced on top of me. He kissed me the same way, passionate as if he loved me as much as I loved him, maybe even more.

I spent the day lying in bed and just reminiscing on the past five years, things I never knew were possible with Bo Bronson. I glanced over my phone noticing the fourteen missed calls from Todd, and I really didn't give a shit. I rolled over to face Bo, and kissed him over and over again.

It was 5:30 and I had to go. I could blow Todd off all day, but there is no way I could it to Jane. I glanced down and saw she had just texted me

See you in a half an hour? Can't wait to hear about your day. P.S. a package came for you.

I hadn't ordered anything, so that was weird. If Bo had I am sure he would have delivered it him to me himself. Oh well, I do love surprises.

"Bo, I have to go. I made plans with Jane for dinner, clearly I don't have to explain to you what will happen if I cancel on her." He pulled me into him and pressed his lips to my forehead. It would take all of my strength to pull away.

"I completely understand, will you spend the night again?" I wanted to say yes, but I knew that I was diving in way too fast, but I also knew that I needed to pace myself.

"Yes, but not tonight. I need to get things done at the apartment, and I have to edit some photos."

"I'll take what I can get with you Bells." He leaned down and kissed me again, I knew it was a subtler invitation to stay but I couldn't. I had to go.

Chapter Eight

I walked up to my apartment door and could hear multiple voices in my apartment. I instinctively tried to listen closer so I knew what I was walking into. I was hoping that it was one of her friends, but I knew there wasn't a chance in hell, since she never brought any friends home, to my home. I braced myself and opened the door. My body stood completely still. I couldn't have been more surprised in my life.

He ran up to me and picked me up. "Iz, I missed you too much I couldn't wait another week." Holy Shit. Jer is here, I have never been more surprised in my life. I kissed his cheek and started to cry. *What is wrong with me?* I think I was just so overcome with everything that has happened in the past three days I couldn't help but feel my emotions spilling over.

"Baby girl, what's wrong? Not happy to see me?" He pulled me in front of him looking me up and down.

"No Jer, I am more than happy to see you." I pulled back into him and squeezed him harder.

"Eh hem. Oh 'Hi Jane, how was your day?' I'm always the third wheel with you two." She huffed with her arms across her chest, much like the spoiled brat that she is.

Jer had only been up to see me one other time, but stayed for a week and he and Jane had a love hate relationship. They bickered constantly, but were forced to be cordial because I wouldn't have it any other way.

"Jane, how was your day?" Jer and I said in unison.

"Well glad you guys asked, I ordered Chinese for all of us for dinner, I thought maybe afterward we could go dancing. I know I sure as hell need it right now. Work sucked."

"You mean you've actually kept a job long enough to have a bad day?" Jer was such a smart ass with her.

"Fuck you Jeremiah." Yikes.

"Yes Jane, we can eat Chinese and then go dancing, in fact I would love to."

I started getting ready while Jer laid on my bed staring past me. He was filling me in on his first year running the bar, my brother and his brother, who apparently got caught with pot by our parents. Funny how my parents never mentioned anything to me, they probably thought I would critique them on their parenting skills, and they were probably right.

Then Jer told me about Melissa, how perfect she is and how she is just as crazy about him. I made a mental note of her full name, so I could Google her later. She was new to town, which made no sense to me, him either by his voice change Everyone in town grew up there, had the same jobs as their parents and stayed, well most everyone.

Our town was almost like the Truman Show; it seemed unrealistic, like the only things that existed in the world were all there. Most everyone never left, me being the exception to the rule, and I guess now Todd too. *Shit.*

We went out to a new club that Jane suggested. She seemed to always know the best spots, and we always had a good time when she was planning the adventure. Jer, Jane and I chatted it up all night. Reminiscing on times that Jane was not a part of, but she didn't mind because she joined in with Jer making fun of me. I laughed myself when Jer told the story of our last New Year's at home.

"Oh. My. God. Jane you won't believe it, she literally had two sips of champagne New Year's Eve because she had to work the next morning and was a paranoid mess. So, I of course laid her clothes out for her, and slept on the couch, since I was drunk and couldn't make the twenty steps to my home. Anyway, she was supposed to be at work at 7am, at 7:30 I looked at the clock as I heard her mumble 'shit. Damnit. Oh hell.' I chuckled to myself realizing that she had never been late in her life, and was sure it wouldn't be a big deal. Next thing I know I hear the front door slam, and I hear her car hit my car!!!" Jane looked at me in surprise that I hadn't shared this story before, and started laughing so hard tears were falling down her face.

"Oh no, it gets better, she called my phone moments later, to tell me she may or may not have hit my car. Then after she gets to work she called me because she forgot to put a bra on!" After Jer told this part of the story I too lost it and was about to pee my pants. All three of us were so happy in that moment, but I had a feeling that something was about to happen. Call it intuition but a moment later I felt a hand on my lower back and lips on my earlobe.

"Cool it Bo." I said without hesitation. "Oh, if that's what you want to call me from now on, I'll go with it." I felt goose bumps all over my body, and I could tell by Jer's face that I should have told him Todd was not only in town, but also all of a sudden had an interest in me.

"So, high school reunion huh?" Todd said nodding at Jer. He went to shake his hand, and Jer shook his head at me and left. Jane gave me a quick glance, trying to figure out if she should follow him or stay with me. I mouthed the words 'stay please' and she walked up next to me, putting her arms around me. I could already hear Jer's words *what are you thinking? He is the biggest whore in our town. He doesn't care about you at all, he just wants to conquer you.*

Knowing that I was in deep shit with Jer already. I decided to stay out with Jane. Todd hung out with us for about an hour, everything after the brief nibble on the ear was G rated. He knew, he went over board, which was obvious from his behavior for the rest of the night. Jane and I danced the night away, and finally decided to wrap it up at 2am. I glanced down at my phone, and saw no calls or messages from Jer. My heart sank. He was always so dramatic, I thought.

"Jane, I think I am going to stay with Bo tonight!"
"What? Are you serious, is this a sober decision?" She looked more smashed than I was.
"Yes, I am serious. I am going to surprise him." I smiled at the image of him snuggled in bed. I love the way he would snuggle up in the oversized down comforter, with one leg hanging out.

I pictured myself snuggled up right in the curves of his arms and legs. I could already smell him, and I surprised myself how much I wanted him in that moment. I closed my eyes and felt the bliss of my buzz fading quickly into the early stages of a hangover. I opened my eyes and saw his door, I knew the New York Taxis were fast, but either this was a record or I fell asleep on the way. Odds are in favor of falling asleep.

I stumbled up the steps and knocked multiple times, I realized that I couldn't remember if he had given me a key or not. *Maybe this was a bad idea.* Once I realized I had knocked about twenty times I turned and sat on the step. I found myself thinking about Bo and I, and where we could end up. Then I felt myself falling into the deep darkness of my usual drunken sleep.

"Bells." I felt a gentle large hand grasping my shoulder, I shoved it off trying to slip happily back into my dreams.

"Bells, what the hell are you doing out here." I looked up and saw Bo, obviously not dressed for bed and I glanced down at my watch and saw that it was 4:30am. *Did he get dressed to answer my knocks? I know I've been down here for at least an hour.* I glanced back up at him with sad eyes.

"Where the hell were you?" I sounded even more irritated than I actually was, a fine combination of attitude and alcohol.

"Bells, I uh···I was out with a friend from work."

"Really Bo? What's her name?" He looked at me and I knew he was about to lie, he's told millions of them before but this was the first time it hurt.

"It was um, Bob you know, remember dark hair?"

I gazed at him waiting for him to redeem himself, waiting for him to pick up my shattered heart on the streets of Manhattan. I felt my eyes start to water, and I stood up, grabbed my fantastic shoes and began to walk away. I felt his hand try to pull me back.

"Don't Bo. Just please don't." I said the words with no emotion, without looking back. I didn't want to know if he was pissed, upset or unaffected because I wanted to believe that he was devastated. I wanted him to finally want me as much as I wanted him.

I walked for what seemed like twenty blocks before I hailed a cab. As I got in, I heard "All by myself," playing on the radio and I let out a sarcastic laugh. I felt like Cher in Clueless, one of my best friends was pissed at me, and now I'm not totally convinced that the guy who finally started to fall for me, actually fell at all. Maybe he sort of stumbled, and then realized and redeemed himself by jumping up and jogging it off.

Finally, I was lying in my bed and the walk up to my apartment was a complete blur. I looked over and saw Jane snoring and drooling on my couch. My eyes wandered the entire apartment looking for Jer, and since this was a studio I realized he was gone.

There will be lots to do in the morning, so I better get some rest tonight. I closed my eyes and drifted off into a temporary relief.

Chapter Nine

I could feel her weight on my bed, and I rolled right back over feeling my head throb. I couldn't face her right now and tell her that she was absolutely right about Bo all along. She swore he was up to no good, and I should be able to tell that just by looking at him. The truth is, it never really mattered to me until now. I never really cared if he lied to be before, because I lied to him too.

I was sure there have been other women for him in the past five years, but I had no interest in knowing. There were no other men for me, only occasional flirting, that is of course if we don't count Todd. *Fuck.*

I needed to face Jane and her wrath now, before I threw up all over myself. As I felt my heartbeat throughout my head I turned and slowly opened my eyes, hoping that the blinds were still closed.

"Jer." It wasn't Jane. He didn't leave. I wrapped my arms quickly around him, hoping he would never leave me.

"Iz, I am so sorry I stormed off like that last night, but here is your chance before I do it again. Tell. Me. Everything."

So, I did. Including the kiss from high school, which I knew he would be three times as angry with me for, but it was worth getting off my shoulders. I cried, and I laughed when telling him about how ironic it felt that Todd was finally pursuing me. Then I told him about everything with Bo, including last night.

"Iz, I'm sorry babe." That's all he said. And in that moment, that's all I wanted to hear anyway. He wrapped his arms around me in the same way I pictured Bo and I. I felt like I was finally home, he smelled like home, like my childhood, a combination of all the worst memories laced with all the best. He was everything, in my past and I realized I could never lie to him again because if nothing else worked out in the world, I would be happy with just him for the rest of my life.

I reached up and kissed him on the cheek, "I love you Jer."

"I love you too Iz." He paused for a moment then asked me the question, which he already knew the answer to. "Come home with me today. I'll cut my New York trip early and bring you home for some extra time away."

"Of course." I felt my heart flutter at the thought. As much as I loved New York City, I missed the simplicity of home.

I jumped out of bed and made my way into the bathroom to get showered and start packing my things. I felt all of the disappointment about Bo drain out of me. I didn't have the energy to be sad about it anymore; I gave myself permission let it go. I came out of the bathroom and saw that Jer had made me my favorite hangover breakfast, cheesesteak!

He looked at me and then stared down at his palm, which was holding my phone. "Iz, don't be mad, but I deleted all of his messages. I don't think you need to hear the excuses right now." I smiled and nodded my head, and then began to scarf down my cheesesteak.

As I was eating my hangover away, I stared at Jer and realized he was more excited than me to go home. I ran my hand through my hair picturing this new love interest of his, and feeling sorry for her that she will never be good enough for him. At least not from my perspective anyway.

"Iz, I can't wait for you to meet her." He totally knew what I was thinking about. *Damnit,* did I really have to be so obvious. I realized I had been making the face of disapproval while nonchalantly eating my cheese steak.

"Yeah, me neither Jer." Well there goes that whole not lying to Jer thing already. "Is your stuff all ready?" He smirked knowing it wasn't, but since I was on such a roll "Of course Jer. I'll meet you down there in five."

I sent Jane a quick text

Change of plans, heading home today. Meet me there on Friday? ~B

Her response was almost instantaneous.

See you then bitch! Good riddance ☺ ~ J

This would be Jane's first time coming to my hometown. She has met my family via Skype, and they love her as much as I do, although she is so disgustingly nice to them, I thought for sure they would see right through her. I think she will be in for quite the shock when she sees exactly how small the town I grew up in is. We've had the discussion hundreds of times, but she never seems to grasp exactly how small.

The conversation always ends with her comparing my home to some sort of hillbilly movie, but she will be quite surprised when she realizes she's right on.

I ran down the steps carrying my two bags, I would have packed more but I was confident that my mother left my room just the way it was, including my closet.

I allowed Jer to drive my car all the way home, so I could sit back and relax. I loved driving in the city, probably because of my control issues, but hated driving on the long boring roads that would take me home.

I felt my phone vibrate and I glanced down with knots in my stomach when I saw his name. I pressed ignore and closed my eyes for the remainder of the trip.

Chapter Ten

I woke up about an hour before we reached our town. Jer's eyes were focused on the road, but I could tell his mind was somewhere else. Then I realized he had his Bluetooth in and was intently listening to someone on the other line.

I was totally trying to pretend to still be asleep but he turned and put his hand on my knee and mouthed 'how was your nap?'

I nodded my head and started to look at all the surroundings that I practically had memorized as a kid. I could close my eyes and come here any time I wanted, from memory.

I smelled the faint, but distinct smell of sea water, and I felt the warmth of the southern sun. I started thinking about my little brother. I wondered what his plans were after college, and I imagined that he would be staying here, even if he had planned otherwise.

I wished that we had more of a relationship then we did, but unfortunately no matter how bad I fought for it, no matter how much I put into it, we were just always on different paths. Red and I didn't even look alike, he used to joke as kids and tell me that I was adopted. Obviously if anyone was adopted it would be him, the only redhead in our family. As much as he annoyed me, being so close to home I began to get excited to see him.

"Yes sweetheart, she just woke up actually so I will have to call you later if that's ok?" Ugh. I am going to throw up, and I doubt that there is any alcohol in my system to blame it on.

"Ok Meliss. We will see you tomorrow." He placed the Bluetooth down and immediately stepped on the gas, almost as if he was racing to get back to her.

"Really Jer? I mean you barely know this girl." I gave him my best teenage girl bitch fit.

"Really Iz, I mean obviously I'm not going to propose or anything but I really feel something with her. I get butterflies. I take that back it sounds

lame. But I do feel something special with her." I could see the sincerity in his eyes.
"Ok Jer, I won't judge until I've met her but so help me···" I crossed my arms and spat the words as if they were poison.
     "I know Iz. That's why I keep you around, I'm sure you already googled her."
Damnit, I've been so caught up with my own soap story that I forgot to look this bitch up. I pulled out my phone to make a light joke and asked him what her last name was.
"Mills. But you won't find anything, I've already looked."
     "Well when was the last time you were a jealous best friend, don't underestimate my powers." I smiled wickedly and started laughing. He knew I was right, if there was anything at all I would be the one to find it.
"So would you like to take a bet on how many?" I said.
"How many what?" He stared at me blankly.
"How many skeletons she has in the closet." I could tell by the look on his face he was now pissed so I changed the subject immediately.
"How are your parents?" I felt like a dog sniffing in the air as we got closer to the ocean. "They are great. No one knows that you are coming home with me early so it will be a nice surprise. They miss you so much Iz, how long has it been anyway?"
     I felt a little guilty when he asked me this question. I had enough money to probably take off a week every month, but I never found a reason to come home in the past five years. My parents know of Bo, but have never met him. They know of my job, yet I don't think they would notice my work if it was on a billboard in their town. They liked to stay where they were and live as if nothing changed. Sometimes I swear that they pretend I just moved down the street.
     It would have probably been easier for me to visit than it was for them to learn skype. I remember calling Jer and asking him, wait begging him to go over and teach them how to skype.

Three hours after he called me and cussed at me jokingly for an hour.

"It's been five years Jer." I said it quietly and he could tell I felt ashamed.

"Iz, we all know you are a hard worker. We are all so proud of you, your parents especially I know they don't tell you much but they are."

We pulled up to a cute cottage that I don't remember as a kid, and I realized that this was Jer's place. I smiled and my body filled up with excitement, I jumped out of the car and ran up to the door.

"Where's my key?" I held out my hand to him.

"Right here honey." He placed the pink key in my hand and I turned the knob slowly.

I think I held my breath until he put his arms around me from behind. I looked around and was completely overwhelmed with how much a place I've never been to in my life, could feel like a home that I made for myself. I broke away from Jer's arms and walked through the living room. It was cozy and smelled as if someone had been baking pies, then I saw the apple pie candle and chuckled. I stood in front of the mantle above the fireplace and it was filled with pictures of Jer and I, and his parents and brother. I felt so happy to be on the shelf next to them, any visitor would assume that I was his sister.

"Do you like it?" He asked already knowing my answer.

"How did I not help you decorate? I obviously did a great job of training you on interior design before I left for the city."

"Let me show you my room."

He opened an oversized wooden door, and I took note of the old door knob. "Is that your old door knob?"

"Yeah. Can't believe you noticed." He was opening the door slowly for a dramatic effect. "Give me a break." I hurried past him and looked into the room. I was in awe.

I looked at the room that was filled with all of my old photography. Before my celebrity clientele I had taken thousands of other photos and Jer had access to them all.

Above his bed was the photograph I had taken the last time I came home five years ago when Jer and I were at the beach. It was under the pier, and after I took the picture I couldn't leave. It was so calming and Jer stayed there with me until the sun went down. I don't think either one of us had said a word to one another. At that time, I was barely surviving in New York, and he was actually bummed that his father had asked him to start taking over the bar. I think that Jer, although he never said it wanted to get away like me, maybe even with me. His Dad had been running the bar since he was twenty-two and decided that he should retire and Jer should continue the family tradition.

"I lay on my bed every night and I can almost close my eyes and feel the breeze on my face, the sand on my feet and smell the ocean." He said it in a smart-ass way.

"No shit Jer this damn house is on the beach." I'd give it right back to him.

I looked at all the other photos, all of which I had taken and it made me miss taking those types of photos. I felt like all of my time went to the highest paying client and I left the love of photography behind with all of the double shifts to survive.

I toured the rest of the house by myself while Jer made us dinner. I decided on surprising my parents in the morning, and I could really use another night to prepare myself for all of the questions that I had dodged for the past five years.

I smelled the stew and snuggled up on the couch and finally glanced down deciding to read some of my text messages. I cautiously opened the phone.

Bells, need to talk. Please just call me back already. ~Bo

And another one…

Why aren't you answering your door? Are you ok? Did you make it home alive?~Bo

I started feeling bad that I didn't at least let him know I was alive. So I sent him a quick one back and then turned my phone off.

I'm alive and well. I won't be in the City for a week, call you when I get back. ~ B

I felt proud that I at least told him that I would call him when I get home. I wasn't completely convinced that I would be ready to hear his excuses then but I couldn't run away from the situation.

I felt the ocean breeze drifting through the living room window and heard the low sound of Jer's voice singing along to a country song in the kitchen. I snuck around the corner to watch him.

He was cutting up veggies and I smiled at how meticulous he still was about everything. I wondered if he was also this way about running the bar. His voice was amazing, although he'd never believed me when I told him that. Jer never sang for anyone beside myself, and I'm quite sure a few girls he dated before. His elementary school teacher told him that he would never be able to carry a tune, and that bitch's opinion still rests on his mind.

"Hey lady. Hope you're hungry I am making tons of food." As I was about to open my mouth to respond that I was starving I saw that he was on the phone, and hadn't even noticed I was spying on him. Jer never let a girl come in between us, not that she was just yet, but surely, she was well on her way. This is not my old Jer, and I have no choice but to change him back.

Chapter Eleven

I walked back into his room and began pacing. I heard the text tone on my cell and glanced down at the text from Jane.

How many pairs of shoes should I bring? I've narrowed it down to ten.

I quickly replied, glad to have my mind drift off to other places for a moment.

Ten is way overboard, don't you remember we don't even wear shoes down here.

I could picture her laughing and it made me smile. I am sure in the end she would bring at least ten pair plus another on her feet upon arrival. She had no idea what she was in for and apparently neither do I.

After barricading myself in his room for about a half hour, I decided I couldn't make a game plan, I had to just ride the wave as Jane used to tell me. I threw on an outrageously adorable shirt dress, no shoes and my long blond hair with loose curls. I threw on a quick nude shade lipstick added some blush and began to make my way into the kitchen.

I sat down on the bench at the island and stared at Jer. His blue eyes stared at me, and I could feel them seep into my soul.

"I'm assuming you heard my conversation with Melissa?" He smiled.

"What makes you think that?" I laughed quietly. He was so on to me.

"The fresh makeup and the short dress." He gave a judging glance.

"Jer, I just want her to be a little bit intimidated by me, that way she will be afraid to hurt you." I couldn't even believe my own lie.

"Iz, whatever you say. Just play nice. And by the way since when has it been you looking out for me? I thought I was the one in charge of worrying." He let out a sigh.

"Maybe I grew up and realized I haven't been worrying enough about you all along." I quickly looked to the door and saw her walk in.

I am sure she immediately noticed me eye her up from head to toe. Not that there was very much of her anyway. She was about 5'2 and only weighed an estimated 95lbs. She seemed innocent and pure, and I felt a wave of guilt run over me. Maybe this could be the girl for him, and I was so judgmental. I now know what it's like to be on this side, and I remembered all the times I stood exactly where she was, knowing I was being judged and reviewed.

"Melissa, I'm Iz, I mean Bella. How are you?" I put my hand out, and she pulled me into a hug. I wasn't one hundred percent sure I wouldn't break her, but I hugged her back anyway. I looked over at Jer who nodded approvingly, maybe even quietly thanking me. I'm not much of a hugger and he knows it.

Melissa and I chatted over dinner and I almost forgot that Jer was in the same room. She seemed so intrigued by my work, and asked if I was able to get her copies of the ones in Jers room. She explained that she was in nursing school, and really enjoyed small town life. She told me how Jer talks to her the entire way to classes, which I gathered was about an hour each way.

I felt as if I was swallowed whole, and she had my complete attention. I looked down at feet ashamed that I judge Jer about falling for her so fast. She was everything that he explained to me and I felt guilty as his best friend that I ever doubted him. My thought process was interrupted thankfully by Melissa's loud laughter. She ran her slender fingers through her honey blond hair and I saw Jer look at her, and I knew that he truly felt that she was amazing.

After dinner we played Trouble, my favorite game as a child. Jer's intention has always been to preserve my childhood, my Peter Pan. I remember when he was 10, the age he first started sneaking into my room. I always thought we were getting one over on my parents, turns out they knew all along.

Jer was sneaking in on the eve of my sixteenth birthday, and decided to spend the night. My Peter Pan made me a tent, brought the flashlights and Trouble. Of course, my parents rushed into my room when then heard the loud popping sound of the plastic dome that held in the dice.

My mom just laughed, and I asked her if she was mad, she replied and told me in six years she never had a problem with him sneaking in my window, and tonight wouldn't be any different. Jer and I laughed so hard we almost peed our pants. Many of our best memories ended with almost peeing our pants.

Melissa was laughing quietly because she was the only one who had no pegs out of home. Jer purposely sent me back on numerous times, to make her feel better. He placed his hand on my lower back, thanking me for being a good sport. I leaned into him for a half way hug, and I felt home. Melissa's eyes quickly shot at me as if to tell me to back off of her man. I felt a stabbing pain in my heart, and pulled away from him.

Melissa seemed like a wonderful woman, and Jer obviously seemed to care for her and for the first time in our friendship, I became the third wheel.

"Jer I'm super tired, I think I'm going to head to bed. Melissa, it was great to meet you." I shook her hand and Jer pulled me in for a kiss on the cheek, though I wasn't looking at her I could tell she was burning a hole through my head. I quietly slipped into my oversized t-shirt, well Jer's t-shirt and headed into his bed. I wondered briefly if he would have an issue with this since he is with Melissa now, then I realized I didn't care either way. I was exhausted and obviously the couch was going to be occupied for a little while. She didn't seem like the type to go down without a fight; she would be here until at least 2am.

I thought it was comical that I was carrying on so well with her, that I never thought that my relationship with Jer would be a little too comfortable for her. Hadn't he emphasized how close we were? Ugh. I have other things to worry about, like Bo. With my stomach now in knots for multiple reasons, I surrendered to sleep.

Chapter Twelve

"Iz, I'm so sorry she acted like that. I explained how close we were and she had nothing to worry about." He wrapped his arms around me, while we both laid in his bed.

"Somehow, I don't think you told her we sleep in the same bed." I exhaled, still half asleep. "Iz, it doesn't matter what she knows. She will never change what we are and what we have, if she does she's gone I swear." He spoke the words with conviction.

I turned to face him, and stared into his gorgeous blue eyes. My eyes glanced down at the tattoo he had on his forearm, *Amor Vincit Omnia, love conquers all*. I remembered being with him when he got that tattoo, and how he said it was for us. It was right before my move to the city and I needed to know that our friendship would make it, that it would remain unscathed. Jer needed it to, which is why I have the same tattoo in much smaller script on my ribs, right next to my heart.

For the first time I wondered if it would always be our love that conquered all, or if maybe a new love would take its place. I do believe in the proverb but I also believe that the only constant in this life is change, and right now I'd do anything to keep us where we are.

"It's fine Jer really, I figured one girl would eventually have something to say about us." I felt defeated.

"Iz, she knows we've never done anything including kissing, she has nothing to say and if she does I'm done. I'm not dealing with it." I saw his temper start to muster its strength.

"Speaking of our significant others, what's the deal with yours, any word?" He was prying, and really good at it.

"I haven't spoken to him Jer, not yet." I almost wished I believed myself, but I knew the conversation I would be having first thing in the morning with Bo. We would probably make up and I would feel guilty for not standing up for myself.

"Jer I have to go to sleep, I'm going to need the rest to deal with my family in the morning." I rolled gracefully back over.

He leaned over and kissed my cheek, and turned to face the other way. I could feel his body lightly twitch and I knew he was asleep. Now that I was awake, sleep wasn't as welcoming as it was three hours ago. I saw two messages on my phone and decided to read them rather than waiting for the morning.

The first was from Jane.

Two more days sass···can't wait to be all country with yall!

My assumptions were that she was wasted and now passed out on my couch, scratch that, bed.

The next was a little more unexpected but I was happy to see it.

Hey Lady. I can't wait to see you in the morning, I'm back in town and rumor has it you are too. If you're free let's do dinner tomorrow at Unc's.

I texted back immediately, without thinking my thoughts through.

Sure Todd. Sounds great. Will be good to see you too.

The thing is about text messaging, once it's sent, you can't take it back. I realized when I clicked send that I would have a lot of explaining to do, not only to Jer but also Bo when we sorted things out. Sick to my stomach again, I turned my phone off and forced myself to fall asleep.

I woke up to the sound of a blender, and knowing what that meant I almost fell out of the bed on my way to the kitchen.

Jer was standing above a bowl licking his fingers; of what I am sure was batter for banana pancakes, my favorite. He smiled and looked a little guilty for licking the bowl. I took a deep breath in, and stared at all of the tattoos covering his chest and down his right arm. Beneath all of them was the sweet boy who used to sneak in my window. Now no one would ever know.

"Mornin' Iz." He said in an exaggerated country accent. I walked up to the bowl and stole it out of his hands, his mouth dropped.

"You know raw eggs are bad for you Jer, I'm saving your life." I dipped my finger in.

"Sometimes you drive me crazy." He chuckled and grabbed the bowl back.

"All the time, you drive me crazy Jer." I whispered into his ear. He looked at me, and I knew I was in trouble.

I ran to the bedroom and tried to shut the door. *Too late.* I saw his hand reach around, and then his head. I ran to the bed and tried to barricade myself under his covers.

"That's it Iz, you're trapped surrender now."

"No way!! No tickling Jer I mean it, we are too old for this shit!" I sounded frustrated, but inside I couldn't wait for him to get me.

I felt his hand on my foot, and I started screaming. I reached up and tickled his side. His laughter filled the room, echoing mine.

After a half an hour of wrestling and tickling, we decided we had worked up enough of an appetite to call a truce. Jer started making breakfast and I made my way to the shower. I closed my eyes as the warm water trickled over me, in this moment I had no worries. I knew however that the moment I opened them, my mind would start driving me crazy again.

"Well it's about time little miss." Jer smiled and put the coffee cup to his lips. I snatched the paper out of his hands.

"Hmmmm···. what's the headline story for today, ahh the crops were damaged in a storm last night." I gave him a quick roll of the eyes "I guess I'm not in Kansas anymore."

"Iz, how soon you forget what it's like to live a normal life, and not read or hear about the 25 homicides that happened in the five hours you were asleep."

Jer was right, I feel like there is so much crime in the city that I've become accustomed to it being the norm. It's nice to come home, refreshing to know there are still places in the world where violence isn't an expected aspect of my morning.

We small talked our way through breakfast, and I informed Jer that I would be meeting Todd at the bar tonight since I knew he was working I couldn't find a way around it. He was calmer than I expected.

"Iz, just be careful ok? Just because you grew up and got some sense doesn't mean the rest of us did." He gave me a hug and wished me the best with my parents and I knew I would need every bit of it.

Chapter Thirteen

I rang the doorbell since my parents weren't expecting me for another day. I never knew if dad would have the gun loaded next to the door and I didn't want to take my chances. I nervously looked down at my phone, anticipating the non-stop calls from Bo, but so far there haven't been any this morning.

I heard my Mother yelling at my father to get the door, and when I saw the doorknob turn my heart skipped a beat. He looked at me for less than a second and I was in his arms. He lifted me up with such ease, it was like I never grew up. "Dad, I missed you so much I could cry." I normally wasn't emotional with my parents on the phone or even through skype, but there is something about physically being near them that makes me homesick.

I heard Mom crying before I could see her, she has always been melodramatic so this was expected.

"I···I···what? How are you here already?" You would think I wasn't due in for another year. "Mom, I came in a little early with Jer, I wanted to surprise you."

"Well you did. Now let's get you inside and cleaned up, you need some product in your hair." Mom would probably scold me if she knew how much product it took to get my hair to look this smooth and flat. I opened the door to my room, and was relieved to know that my assumptions were correct that even though I had been gone for five years, nothing changed.

Visiting my room was not just going to a physical place, but transporting myself to another time. I fell onto my bed and inhaled the soft scent of my Mother's laundry detergent, which also hasn't changed. I could even assume that she probably still changes my sheets once a week.

My Mother never liked change, which is why even though I left she almost pretended I didn't. Although I haven't been around to witness her inability to relax I've got enough witnesses to know better. I heard the knock on my door and smile.

"Honey, it's Mom can I come in?"
"Yes Mom of course, this is your house you know." I would have never breathed these words if I were still sixteen.

"Well honey, I just thought we should catch up. How is that Bo boy? What a peculiar name that is. Well anyway you know Red is graduating and honey I just don't know what to do with myself. Your father hardly eats anything, I mean who am I supposed to feed? I only know how to cook for four and thank goodness your brother has been dating otherwise your food would be wasted." She went on and on. I glanced at my watch and noticed that it had been well over an hour by the time we decided to make our way to the living room.

I can tell that even though she doesn't have to work or worry, that is all that she allows herself to do at home. At least Red is still dependent enough to make her feel useful. I'll have to remind Jer to come over more often and make sure she doesn't lose her social skills.

I feel like my parents have been together so long that they don't even need to actually speak to know what the other is thinking. They constantly exchange looks and then shake their heads at one another as if they were both telepathic. My father has always been the quiet one, which I am thankful for because if everyone knew how much knowledge he has to lend, I would be at the end of a very long line. I am so blessed that I have always been the first.

Even though I know my father would never breath the words to me, his heart aches that I am not married with kids yet. I think maybe he has even given up hope on me and instead assigned that role to my brother. Which reminds me, yet another girlfriend I have yet to meet this week, and again I already can't stand.

Red has been with this one for about a year now, and I obviously haven't met her. I am definitely guilty of judging a book by its cover in this case, but it is my little brother I am concerned for. I've always wanted a sister, and since I don't have a choice this late in life I settled for Jane. Although I have no interest in where this girl came from or what she plans on doing in life, I can bet that my mother will make sure we are best friends after this weekend.

"Honey, do you need something to eat?" Mom peeked her head into the door.
"I'm good Ma, going to Unc's tonight." She nodded and shut the door. Just as it was completely closed it re-opened. "Oh and honey don't forget tomorrow Morning we will be having brunch with Jessie, your brother's girlfriend. It will be so much fun." Her voice disappears into the hallway and I know she can visualize me rolling my eyes. *Funny* I even act like a teenager when I am back home, there must be something about this room.

I began laying out clothing options for this evening on my bed. I was tempted to bring all my city clothes with me, but I knew I'd stick out and Jer would be making fun of me. He is aware of both sides of me, my city alter ego and the country girl from next door, and although mentally I always feel the same two pictures side by side you would think I am the separated twins from the parent trap.

I had decided on a plain white t-shirt and dark denim jeans with a pair of Tori Burch flats. I had to bring a little part of the city to the south. I had texted Todd to meet me at Unc's and Jer would already be there working so I could let him obviously watch over me all night long.

As I pulled up to Unc's, I realized that nothing had changed. I often miss that aspect when I am in the city. I saw Jer's truck out pack and decided to park next to him, I've acquired the skill of judging cars to park next to from the city.

I walked in the back entrance and ran into Jer. His crystal blue eyes lit up, seemingly in disbelief that I was actually here.

"Iz, I just made some fried tomato if you want to sneak some back here before you go out. I know you have this skinny girl rep to keep up with, I wouldn't want them to see the fatty within." He chuckled and handed me the contraband.

"Is he here yet?" I asked, finding myself a little nervous especially now that we are on his turf.

"been looking at the door every five minutes for the past hour and a half." He smacked my butt and pushed me toward the door.

As I walked in I saw many familiar faces with names that I couldn't recall. I don't think I would have a problem with anyone being able to recognize me, so I could skip over all of the reintroductions.

"There's my girl." I felt Todd's hand slip around my waist.

"Hey···where's my drink?" I suddenly felt like alcohol was a must.

I turned to the bar and saw Jer making me a Bacardi and coke and felt a little bit relieved. I was socializing with Todd, ok more like flirting with Todd and I loved it. I felt amazing that he was so into me, hanging on my every word and not taking his eyes off of me for a second.

I confessed everything to him about Bo, and he comforted me in a way that I would have thought of as taking advantage had I been sober. At least I knew that Jer wouldn't let it get too out of hand. I looked over and saw about ten girls ordering drinks and giving him their numbers. They were clearly sloshed and out for a bachelorette party, I gathered from the penis necklaces and tiara. Jer looked like a guy that would go home with any of these women in a second, and would be out before their husbands had any suspicion. Luckily for their husbands, Jer was such a classy guy.

I saw the maid of honor reach over the bar and lick his face. Before I could even register what, I was doing I walked behind the bar and came up behind Jer.

"Sorry Ladies, hands off he's taken." I turned to him and kissed him on the lips, nothing more nothing less, and turned to go back to Todd.

I heard the girls gasp and I looked back to see the smirk on Jer's face. Todd was confused about what just happened, but as everyone typically did he wrote us off as being nothing more than friends and moved on.

Three hours later Todd was on his way out and offered me a ride, I politely declined to spend more time with Jer. Before I knew it, this week would be over and it would probably be another year before I saw him.

"Hey Iz, the bar is getting ready to close how about I pack us up a few and go to the pier." He was already packing the cooler, and already knew my answer. About an hour later after I helped him clean up the bar we got into the truck and headed to the beach. I had the window all the way down, and was singing my heart out to Miranda Lambert.

"Awe now Iz, what do you think all of your city friends would think about this behavior, you're one breakup short of being a real-life country song."

I could see the pier and started to get butterflies in my stomach. So many places had changed, yet my home would always be the same and it seemed that I could also go back to being the teenager who would sneak down here with her best friend.

I felt my feet hit the sand before the truck was completely stopped and I could hear Jer running behind me. I ran into the crashing waves and felt him splash behind me. There was no man-made light, no honking taxis, no polluted air just me my best friend and the ocean.

After about 20 minutes and being completely saturated we sat underneath the pier and started drinking. I glanced over at Jer and his chiseled abs, tattooed arms and amazing smile.

"Jer, how come it was never us?" It was too late to take it back, and I had too many drinks to care.

"I think we love each other too much." He laid his head on my shoulder, and emotions overwhelmed me.

"I miss you Jer, every single day I miss you." I felt the tears starting to fall, and I could tell he noticed them. He placed his hand gently on my chin.

"Izabella, you know that when you need me I am there. I have never once not been there for you, but we grew up you know? We have to be apart to make us appreciate each other more."

"I love you Jer." I said the words with my eyes closed, and even though I've said them many times before they felt different this time. What also felt different was Jer's lips on mine.

I felt myself kissing him back, and it was nothing like the innocent kiss from earlier tonight. I felt his tongue slip into my mouth and his arms pulling at my shirt. Although Jer had a number of times seen me in my bra and underwear, this time was on a whole new level. He pulled away from my lips only to take my shirt over top of my head. My pink lace boy short panties were already exposed before we went into the ocean.

I was laying on the sand looking up at him, staring into his eyes aware that we were both intoxicated, and this may be a mistake but simultaneously aware that we have been in this same situation fully clothed and never kissing millions of times before.

I wanted to pause this moment and over analyze the situation. Figure out what changed between us, to make this happen now. While debating if I should stop this before we went any further I felt his lips on mine again. I felt him run his fingers through my long blond sandy hair. He kissed me with a hand on my face, my favorite way to be kissed. He was passionate, and I matched him step for step along the way.

We had to be lying on the beach for hours, never going any further physically than kissing, but emotionally I had gone over the edge.

"Iz, I think we need to go back to my place." I nodded in agreement. We drove home and it was as if nothing had happened. We laughed about the bachelorette party and how after the bar closed Jer showed me a drawer full of phone numbers he had accumulated since taking over the bar.

We pulled up to his house and I ran to the door pulling out my pink key. "Honey we're home!" He jokingly shoved past me.

"Yeah, well I call shotgun on the shower." I yelled behind him.

I ran into the bathroom first and was trying to hold the door shut with all of my strength as he pushed on the other side.

"You better let me in Iz!!!" I could barely make out his words through his laughter. Finally, I held the door in place long enough to get it locked and I quickly jumped in the shower.

I felt the sand gritty in the bottom of the shower, and although I strongly disliked the feeling, it brought back a flood of wonderful memories.

I had my eyes closed picturing all the parties, and bonfires on the beach as a teenager and all the memories Jer and I had already made under the pier. I had no idea what to say to Jer in the morning when we both sobered up, and right now I had no more intentions to worry about it.

As I was about to open my eyes I felt two hands push my hair to the side. I felt every single finger traveling down my spine. I turned over my shoulder and saw him standing there, and realized I never knew how perfect his body was. His face was completely serious, and his blue eyes wouldn't part from mine. He reached down and grabbed my hand.

"Jer what the hell are you doing in here?"

"Like I've never seen you naked before Iz."

"You've never seen me naked after making out for an hour on a beach in the dark."

"You win." He turned me forward and pressed me against the cool tiles and started kissing me again. With one arm he moved the showerhead so the water was pouring onto me to keep me warm.

His kiss became more intense and he pulled away. "I really love you Iz, you know, that right?" I nodded my head, and pulled him back into me.

I felt his skin pressed completely against mine, and as he pressed his hands to my chest I let out a sigh. This is as far as we would go for the rest of the night, but we stayed there for quite a while.

I woke up and felt as though I had a full night's rest, but by glancing at the clock it had only been two hours. I rolled over and saw Jer's bare ass and decided I needed some coffee before we addressed last night.

Tomorrow Jane was coming down and hopefully I would figure out what happened between Jer and I before then. I grabbed a sweater and sat on the porch with my coffee accompanied by the early morning chill. I heard Jer get out of bed and got knots in my stomach.

"Morning lady." He said as he took a seat next to me. I watched the steam hover over the water and took a deep breath in.

"About last night⋯." Someone needed to address this issue. Just then I heard my phone ring.

"I'll grab it for you, just in case it's Jane." I knew it wouldn't be, it was too early for Jane. He jumped up and ran into the room. I heard him lower his voice and couldn't make out every word so I tip toed outside of the room.

"Well Bo, I'm sorry for your loss but like I said she moved on. He's a great guy and I totally approve so⋯. yeah⋯. ok⋯well I don't know if you can compete with him but good luck trying you lying cheating bastard." He slammed the phone and I ran back to the porch.

"You do realize that you walk like you weigh 300 pounds right?"

"What do you mean?"

"I heard you eavesdropping, lady. Lets just say the rest of your trip will be a little more relaxing with Bo not bothering you."

"Yeah well I guess my new guy is going to be occupying a lot of my time then." I nudged his side.

Jer started laughing "Oh sorry I just couldn't think of anything else to get him off your back, so I guess the field is wide open for Todd now." I was confused by what Jer was implying, and what happened between us last night. I know that he wasn't that far gone that he didn't remember what happened, but I did know him well enough to know that he wasn't ready to talk about it.

"Jer you know there is nothing going on between Todd and I right?"

"Well you should give him a shot, you have been waiting your whole life for him." He winked at me and took another sip of his coffee.

I will give Jer until tonight until I force him to tell me exactly what was going through his head. I guess I would also have to tell him what was going through mine, that I started to picture us as a couple somewhere in between the beach in the shower I found myself falling in love with a man that I had already loved for years.

Jer grabbed his phone out of his pocket and answered, interrupting my thoughts.

"Hey babe⋯.yeah I'll meet you over at my parents in a few hours to help set up for the party. Ok⋯.you too."

"Who was that?" I asked a little too snippy than I would have liked.

"Melissa. She is going to help us set up at my parents, remember they are having the boys dinner tonight to celebrate."

"Oh right, I can't believe this week is flying by and they graduate tomorrow."

"So are you still planning on going back to the city Sunday?"

"I don't know why I would stay here? I mean I love visiting but I have to go back to work right?"

"Are you asking me if I want you to stay?" He said surprised.

"No. I'm leaving Sunday." What I really wanted to scream was *yes, ask me to stay here with you. Tell me you felt it too and it wasn't just a drunken hookup.* But instead, he stood up and refilled his coffee cup. I got up with a clear attitude, my running shoes and stomped outside.

My parent's house was only three miles away so I decided to just run, and with any luck I would make it in time for breakfast. On the way I forced myself to think of something other than what happened last night. I had to pretend it didn't happen because Jer is my rock and I can't afford to lose him right now. He is my calm in my chaos, or at least he was my calm.

Chapter Fourteen

I could see my mother peeking around the curtains as I rounded the last curve in the road before our home. I assumed that Jessie hadn't made it over yet, and that is whom my mother was looking out for. I noticed her brief smile and then disappear behind the curtains. She then appeared in the door and almost seemed to be running as fast as me. I know that my mother at this point in her life needed me to be here this weekend, and I felt I owed it to her for being such a pain in the ass teenager.

I knew that my mother could very easily read my emotions, and it was crucial that I not allow her any insight on what just happened between Jer and I.

"Hun, I didn't think you were coming until later···.I'm assuming you'll be taking a shower here before we go to brunch?"

"I will Ma, and just in case that was a question not a statement I was already planning on showering."

"Oh, I am just so happy you're here. You'll love little Jessie, such a southern belle."

I sighed in a deep breath; so not ready to deal with all of the fake smiles I would be putting on today. I then remembered that Jane was coming in shortly, and I actually didn't have to force a smile after all.

After my shower I glanced at my phone to see three messages from Jer, I realized that in a matter of two weeks I've managed to ignore two of the men in my life. Unfortunately, I don't have many left.

I heard a light knocking on the door, before I could mumble a response the door was pushed in and my little, or should I say big brother came in and wrapped his arms around me. Though we were never very close, there was still an unspoken bond between us. I looked up at him jokingly "Hello big brother."

"Hey Sis, how's it hanging?"

"Good. I'm actually pretty excited to dine with this little gal of yours this morning." I said with my best memory of my old accent.

"yeah yeah yeah···.you can take the girl out of the country. Anyway you'll be at Jason's tonight for the dinner thing for us right?"

"Of course, that is why I drove all the way down here right?"

"Yeah, too bad you can't stay longer. Now I'll have to wait another 5 years to see you."

"Oh shut up and stop making me feel guilty. I'll make it up to you come see me in New York next month when things settle down."

"Alright B. Catch you later tonight. Be nice to my lady."

As he left I could hear him greet his girlfriend so I knew I had to throw myself together quickly. In five minutes after I looked halfway presentable I put my fake smile on and walked out into the living room.

My Mother had her arm around Jessie, as if they had been friends for years.

After brief introductions, and some corny jokes from my mother we were on our way out the door. I was shutting my door when I heard it. Two long slow honks followed by···

"B I MADE IT!!!!!!"

I turned to see my very best friend, and the relief I had momentarily experienced was drained when I saw him sitting in the passenger seat.

I knew Jane could see the rage on my face as I caught my first glimpse of Bo.

"Before you get all pissy, let me explain." She was halfway to my mom's car when I shut the door and rolled the window down.

" I have to go to brunch with my Mom. You better have five good reasons why I shouldn't kill you when I get back. Start brainstorming."

"Got it." She winked at me and smiled.

Maybe she knows something I don't. Bo hadn't said a word to me, or attempted to make eye contact. He reminded me of a puppy that knew he was in trouble and wanted to punish himself. Well at least spending the next hour and a half with Jessie will allow me to focus on something other than my ex just arriving, and my best friend acting like nothing had happened between us.

After all the small talk and stuffing my face, Jessie excused herself which gave my mother the perfect opening to ask me about Bo. She was so excited I had arranged to bring him home, and I wasn't quite ready to ruin it for her. She was already raving about how gorgeous he was in person, and I had to agree with her. Although I could tell that our time apart hadn't treated him well. He could pull any look off. I am pretty confident, and though this one was new I enjoyed it just as much as the others.

I learned almost everything there is to know about Jessie, including how she always had a crush on my little brother. She was also excited that I was a celebrity, and I didn't want to let her down either so I let that one slide.

As my anxiety reached a new high we pulled back up to the house, and I saw Bo sitting in dark denim jeans, and a plain white t-shirt on my porch. I felt the tugging at my heart. At this moment he was completely irresistible to me. I got out of the car and ran to him. He picked me up and I knew he could hear me start to cry. I felt him place his hand on the back of my head.
"It's ok baby, I'm here now."

Chapter Fifteen

"Bells, I've missed you so much."
"I don't forgive you Bo." I whispered into his ear.
"I know, I'll explain later."
"I don't want you to." I whispered again.

I wasn't ready to hear explanations, or excuses. I just grasped on to the fact that he was here in front of me, totally out of his element. He was chasing after me, and it felt so good.

Mom came up behind me. I could hear the excitement in her voice "Bo, hun we are so excited to have you down finally." I quickly wiped the tears away from my eyes.

He reached out and grabbed her hand to place a kiss on it. She glanced over at me and winked, I could see that Bo was planning on sticking around for the whole weekend.

"Well you guys should go get settled in, show them around tell Izabella, take them to Jer's place." I could feel mom's urge to get us out of the house. She had a ton of cooking for the party tonight, so I didn't blame her, and she knew I was not a chef by any means.

"Do you forgive me yet? I mean how hot is he in those jeans?" Jane wrapped her arms around my neck.
" I forgive you. But for all the wrong reasons." I hugged her back and we headed into the house.
"So what are we doing today?" Jane wanted to get drunk; I've seen that look too many times to not recognize it.
" I guess we can go to Jer's bar, but I'll have to fill you in on something later."
"Can't wait⋯.I'll be ready soon." She disappeared into the guest room.
"Bells, we should probably talk." I felt Bo behind me. I turned to face him.
"Bo, I'm not ready to hear it, whatever excuse there is won't be good enough. But here you are, out in the middle of nowhere, wanting to be with me, and for now that's enough."

He leaned in to kiss me, and grabbed the back of my head. It was one of the most passionate kisses I had ever experienced, and while I was kissing him Jer was completely absent from my mind.

He followed me into my childhood room and sat on my bed as I rummaged through the closet. "I can't believe how different I pictured your room."
"I can't believe how sexy you look on a bed covered in stuffed animals."
I felt him come up behind me, and he placed his hands around my waist. I leaned back into him trying not to want him as badly as I did.

I felt his hand unbutton my jeans, and I turned to face him.
"Bo, please don't break my heart. Don't give me a reason to hate you."
"I promise you, you'll break mine first."

I fell onto Bo, and surrounded by my childhood I made love to an amazing man.

<u>Chapter Sixteen</u>

We all piled into the car and headed to the bar. I assured mom that we would meet her at the dinner, and also promised to not be hammered. I had good intentions to keep both promises.

Jane and I both looked like we belonged back in the city with our wardrobes; Bo decided to stay in his jeans and t shirt, and it fitted him more that I thought possible. He seemed to belong here more than we did.

After last night, the last person I wanted to see was Jer. I thought for certain that he would be at his Mom's prepping for the party, but as we pulled in I saw his truck.

I got out of the car and Bo pulled me aside. "Listen, I don't think your friend Jer is too keen on me right now, do you think that we should just head to the party?"
"Well Bo, we are shit out of luck because he is going to be there too. Might as well bite the bullet now." He slid his hand around my waist and we walked in.

Jane walked in first and every face turned to see her. She loved the attention and immediately started playing pool with some of the locals. Bo and I walked over to the bar, I could see the disgust in Jer's face, and for a second I wanted to take up Bo's offer.

"Hey Bud, can we get two of the ladies' favorites." Bo tried to pretend that the call between them never happened.
"Yes and I am not your bud."
"As for you Iz, we will talk later." He went to turn.
" I'm not your child Jer." I snapped back. He looked over his shoulder and shook his head. I couldn't help but take a quick look at his perfect ass, which I had never noticed until last night.

I just couldn't seem to wrap my head around the fact that he was upset with me for getting back with Bo after what happened between us last night. He was being such a hypocrite, and as much as I wanted to scream that at him I decided to take Bo to the dance floor instead.

I felt like I was seventeen again, except instead of being just Iz, I felt like the belle of the ball, or maybe belle of the bar is more fitting. I had Bo put a line dancing song on the jukebox, and Jane immediately found me and started screaming. Two years ago on a drunken night at my apartment I taught her how to line dance, and I was sure she never thought she would use that skill again.

"Shut up!!!! I remember." She picked me off the floor laughing hysterically. I realized that half of my promise to show up to the dinner sober was already broken.

We stayed at the bar for about four hours. Jane made new friends, and hardly paid any attention to me after the line dance, which was fine because I was not in the mood to divulge in my recent scandal. She was exchanging numbers as I was dragging her into the car.

"Jane, we have to go." Bo was already in the driver's seat ready to go.

"I'm coming, I'm coming." I didn't see Jer leave, but I wasn't paying much attention to him after I got onto the dance floor.

Finally Jane was settled into her seat, and was much more sober than I would have given her credit for. Bo placed his hand on my leg and I glanced up at him, this man looked so beautiful. Surely he could do no wrong to me, not now. After finally making the commitment, it just wouldn't make sense. I knew there was a bigger story.

As we pulled up to the party I saw my mother run for the car. Jane was already halfway out of the car before we were even in the park. I shot her a look and she replied "What? I'm like a celebrity down here. The fans are waiting for me." She was truly a gem.

"Honey, oh I'm just so glad you are here. Everyone is dying to meet him." She glanced over bashfully at Bo. I rolled my eyes, I could only imagine what she has been telling everyone about him. I'm sure she started with tall, dark and handsome, which was all 100% correct.

We walked into the back yard, where it was decorated beautifully and strung with lights. It looked like something out of a movie. Jer's mother was always amazing at decorating, but tonight she outdid herself. I knew plenty of girls that would kill to have a wedding here, including me.

"Hi Mrs. Jones, this looks amazing." She wrapped her arms tightly around me.

"My little Iz, you have grown so much, and who might this be?"

I introduced Bo to everyone. I also took notice that Jer and Melissa weren't here yet. I tried to stay focused on the party, but I could feel the tension building up knowing that they would be here any minute.

We went our separate ways, and I saw Bo talking to my brother. Red looked over at me and I smiled at him. He nodded and winked, and I felt really lucky to have him in my life. I also made a mental note to make more time for him.

Maybe it was the age difference, or maybe the fact that we looked nothing alike. Maybe it was that we were nothing alike, but I had to stop making excuses for not being there for him. I remembered him being a little chunk with braces, and I almost can't believe that he turned into a man, well boy man. His red hair turned more of a strawberry blond as he got older and it seemed to suit him much better. His blue eyes, contrasted my brown and his fair skin paled in comparison to my dark olive skin. If I wasn't old enough to remember my mom being pregnant with him, I could almost swear that we weren't related.

I saw him rubbing his earlobe as he was talking to Bo, and I felt comforting warmth knowing that there are some things that we do have in common. I am sure Bo picked up on it too; it was one of my nervous tendencies that he always noticed.

Jason came up and planted a big kiss on my cheek.

"What's up sis?" Jason always called me sis, never by my real name.

"Just celebrating two of my favorite boys tonight…..."
"You're so corny, hey can you introduce me to your friend?"
"Who Bo?"
"Is Bo the hot one with the short skirt and heels?" He raised his eyebrows at me.
"That would be a no, and a hell no to introducing you to her, she's too old, don't even think about it."
"Well I just want a picture of us to show my friends, don't be a bitch."

I punched him playfully in the arm. He was so opposite of his brother. We began catching up, he told me about all the girls he conquered in high school, I told him I was not impressed, although actually I kind of was. He and my brother were best friends and the 'it' boys, according to them. They had no idea that the world didn't revolve around them yet. He started losing my attention as I dazed off staring at Bo, then he said it, and I was sure he saw my reaction.

"So have you met Melissa? Jer says she's the one."
"Yeah. I've met her, she seems great." I put my drink down and walked into the front yard. Jason didn't follow me. I needed a moment to get myself together. Just as I sat on the porch and started to feel the tears building up I heard his voice. I quickly wiped my eyes as they rounded the corner. She had her fingers laced in his, and she looked perfect. Her hair was down and wavy and she had on a floral dress with cowgirl boots. They did look perfect together. I almost couldn't stand myself that I wasn't happy for him. My whole life I've wanted him to be nothing but happy, yet here I was being selfish and hateful.

"Hey guys! So glad you're finally here." I tried to sound as normal as possible.
"Hey Iz." He nodded. I saw him grab her hand a little tighter.
"Hey Izzie, how are you?" I swore she knew I hated to be called that.

"I'm good Melissa. Thanks for asking. The party is beautiful, you guys should go check it out."
"I know, I told Mrs. Jones this would be a beautiful place for a wedding." She nudged Jer in the side and I thought I was going to be sick.
"Are you coming out back?" She asked in the most sickening sweet voice.
"Yeah, I'll be back in a few minutes."
         She leaned into Jer and they disappeared into the back yard.
And that was it. They headed into the back yard as I continued to get composed. I just couldn't get over everything that had transpired in the last week, between Bo cheating on me, or not, me definitely hooking up with Jer and now Jer with his future wife. I felt like my entire world was falling apart, or maybe it was falling together. I lost all control of everything around me and I finally had a grip on that. I stood up and I felt someone grab my arm behind me, instinctively I pulled away.
         "Iz, what the hell is going on with you and why the hell is he here? He cheated on you and has treated you like shit."
         I turned to face him; I could see that he was angry, which fueled my fire. He didn't look concerned the least bit when he walked in with Melissa on his arm.
"Hmmm Jer I wonder what the hell is going on here? Were you not present last night? Was that not you making out with me? Rubbing your hands all over me? Was that a dream?"
"No, it happened." He was staring at the floor.
"Bo showed up this morning and I decided to let him stay, turns out the same applied for Melissa. Last night was a mistake."
"Have you told her about last night?"
"No, and I can bet you haven't told him either. Not that he has the right to know."
"Jer, there comes a time where we need to let go of each other. I think last night was it."
         I could hear him take a deep breath in, I was fully prepared to let him preach to me, but then all loyalty I felt to him disappeared.

I turned and walked into the back yard, I needed to be in front of an audience so he couldn't make a scene, I didn't need the knife to be twisted in my back, I was just getting used to the pain of it being there in the first place. Jer and I never fought like this; I should have never let it get out of hand last night, and neither should he.

I found Bo and gently placed my head on him, he was comfortable and safe, at least at this point in time. As much as I believed that Bo was with someone else, I also believed he would never hurt me. It wasn't in his nature. He looked down at me and winked, I think he could tell something was off.

We continued to make our rounds. Finally it was my Dad's turn to question Bo.

"Well Bo, we've heard a lot about you." He put his hand out to shake my fathers, my Dad kept his tight lipped smile and reached his hand out in return.

"You should be good to my daughter Bo, you should also know that I have a lot of guns." I couldn't help but let out a hysterical laugh.

"What?" My Dad looked at me annoyed.

"You have been waiting to use that line for years!"

"You don't have to worry sir, I have no intentions of hurting your daughter." He grabbed my hand.

"Well in that case you should put a ring on her finger." I know my Dad saw my jaw drop, it was partially because I couldn't believe what he just said and partially because I saw Jer right behind him. By the look on Jer's face I was sure that he heard everything.

"Sorry baby girl, just needed to voice my opinion, seems like you got a keeper here."

"Hey Pops." Jer put an arm around my father. He never called him Pops, so I knew that he was drinking, and trying to scare Bo.

"Hey Jer, good to see you son, have you met Bo?"

"Have I met him? Of course! I'm also the one that Iz came running to when he cheated on her."

"Jer, shut up." This would be my last warning.

"What? You didn't tell everyone that Mr. Perfect is really an asshole?"

"Hunny." My Dad looked at me with pity.

"Dad, it's not true and Jer is drunk."

Thankfully Bo stepped in. "Sir, as I just promised you I will never hurt your daughter. In fact, I was going to wait until later this weekend but I wanted to ask your permission for her to move in with me."

I couldn't read Dad, and that was something that scared me. Fortunately Mom came up and changed the subject.

"Rich, did you know that Bo here is amazing at pool? Lets all go to Unc's after the dinner!"

"Yeah, that should be fun." He looked at Bo sizing him up.

"And by the way Bo, she is a grown woman, she can live wherever she pleases." He shook his hand again and turned away.

"Don't come running to me when he fucks up again." Jer shoved past Bo.

"Bells, I don't know how long I can go without punching him in the face. And I really need to tell you the truth, I promise you I didn't cheat on you."

"Bo, I believe you. I don't need an explanation, not right now anyway."

"Yeah, but I don't think you do believe me."

"Bo, shut the hell up."

"Ok, but you just tell me when."

I was now stressed about the fact that we would have to go back to Unc's tonight. I was trying to calculate in my head how much Jer was drinking and add up the time we had until the dinner was over.

According to my calculations, it was going to be a very long, very verbal night at Uncs.

I saw Jer come back out with the cake, and he avoided eye contact with me completely. We spent the last two hours socializing with all of my old acquaintances, and Bo actually seemed interested in all the stories they had to share about me. He kept his hands placed around my waist the whole night, and it quickly became our comfort zone. Jane was MIA and sent me a text that she would meet me at my house later. I would worry under normal circumstances, but this was far from normal circumstances.

As we started to say our goodbyes, Jer bumped into me.

"We need to talk." He whispered into my ear.

He reached out for my wrist and Bo looked at him disapprovingly.

"Anything I can help you with Jeremy?" Bo said through his teeth. I could feel his arms tighten around me.

"No man, have a good night." He let go, and I saw a glimpse of sadness before the anger surfaced.

"Do you want to explain to me what is going on between the two of you?"

"Not really Bo, it might have something to do with you being here though."

"I figured as much. Let's get going baby." He placed a kiss on my forehead and I felt my eyes start to well up with tears.

"Why don't you head over to the bar, I'm going to help clean up and I'll meet you there in a few."

"Are you sure? I can stay and help."

"No, Dad is expecting you, and I fully expect you to get on his good side, oh and don't beat him in the pool."

"Alright baby, see you in a few."

I went around back and saw Mrs. Jones and Melissa carrying leftovers into the house. I walked to the edge of the yard and looked out over the water. It was hard to imagine that the stars were in the New York sky I was used to. I felt like I was in a place where magic still existed.

I sat down under the huge tree that was decorated with little white lights. I felt defeated, and confused.

"Iz." I heard him creeping up behind me.

"Jer please go away."

"Are you crying?"

"No, I said leave me alone."

"We aren't thirteen anymore, you can't tell me to go away and expect me to listen."

"Jer, what the fuck? Did last night happen? I'm being serious, because just tell me it didn't and we can just go on like it never happened."
"It happened." He put his arm around me.
"I don't know why it happened, or why I did that to you, but I need to tell you something." I looked up at him, waiting to hear the words that I never thought I would be craving to hear from him.

"Iz, I think I am going to marry her." With every attempt to hold myself together, I lost.
"Get away from me." I got up and started sprinting to the front of the house.
"Iz, are you kidding me." He was gaining on me, and I knew that he was faster.
He grabbed my shoulders and pulled me back. " I thought you would be happy for me, she is great! She loves me, and she will take care of me. What the hell is wrong with you?"
"Jer, how can you possibly feel that way about her when last night we were naked in your shower together. We were with each other."
"Iz, I was drunk and so were you. I am so sorry."
"Well since we are being honest, I am moving in with Bo." I said it just to be spiteful, because I really wasn't sure of that decision yet.
"Iz, I don't really care if you screw up your life with him. I know that I'll be happy, and my life will go on without you."
I felt the air escape my lungs, and I turned to walk away. Jer didn't come after me. The bar wasn't far so I just decided to walk and clear my head.
When I opened the door, I saw everyone that I love laughing and getting along like old friends.
My Dad had his arm around Bo, and my heart was momentarily happy.
Both of those men loved me, and that should be enough.
" Hey, you're finally here!" Dad yelled from across the room.

"Oh my gosh Izzie, that guy of yours is so gorgeous! They must really make them better in the city." Jessica, an old frenemy from high school had nothing to hold back.

"Thanks, I really lucked out with him. They aren't all that well groomed."

The bar was packed with old familiar faces, and I decided to drink my way through the night.

Jane finally showed up to the bar, and Jason was right behind her.

"Bells, this little boy has been following me around like a puppy all night."

I laughed and decided to forget everything with Jane. This is what we would have done if we had been in the city, and twenty years old. Although sometimes I felt a little too old to be taking as many shots as I thought I could manage, part of me felt like if I drank enough I could just go back to being that 20 year old innocent girl again.

After my sixth shot, I felt like I almost couldn't stand. It had been awhile since I drank that way, and now I was reminded of why I had waited so long again. Just when I almost fell I heard a loud smack. "Fuck." I said it without even turning around.

I expected to find one of the high schooler's on the floor. As I slowly turned around, I saw Jer holding his nose, and blood pouring out.

"What the hell?" I ran over and saw Bo holding his hand.

"Bo are you fucking kidding me?" I stared at him.

"Trust me Bells, you'll be thanking me when you hear what he said about you."

I looked at Jer, and didn't feel sorry for him at all.

I bent over and handed him a rag. "Goodbye Jer." I kissed his forehead and walked out of the bar.

"Bells, I really am sorry. I just couldn't handle it anymore."

"I don't blame you Bo. It's fine."

"Do you want to know what he said?"

"No, I really can't handle anything else right now."

"Are you ready to go?"

I looked at him opening the door for me. How did I find him?
"Looks like you already know my answer."
He grabbed my hand and sat me in the car.

As soon as I put my seatbelt on, I realized I couldn't hold it in any longer. I started to sob. Bo grabbed my hand and whispered, "I'm so sorry. If I didn't think you were worth the fight I wouldn't be here right now."
I had myself wondering if I really was worth the fight, to Jeremy or Bo. Would Jer really fight for me at the end of the day? Tonight, that answer was no.
"Let's just go home Bo."
"Ok."
"No, not my home here. Our home in the city, I want to go home."
"Bells, your family might be upset they didn't get to say goodbye and what about Jane?"
"I'll leave my mom a note, trust me she will understand. And I'll call Jane and ask her to drive my car back home. I just need to be home."
Bo quietly nodded his head and pulled into my parents driveway. "Do you want me to help you pack up?"
"No I'll just be a minute, most of my stuff is at Jer's and I can just have him overnight it."
"ok, I'll be here waiting for you." I always hoped to hear those words come out of his mouth.

Chapter Seventeen

I scribbled my mom a note on a post it, along with a line about her coming to the city. I feel like if I could get her into the city for a weekend, she would fall in love with it just like I had. I am sure after what they just witnessed they would completely understand me leaving so abruptly.

I went into my room to gather my belongings and I realized everything was at Jer's, and I knew I had to go back tonight. At least I had Bo on my side.

I took in one last deep breath and let the smell of my childhood home consume me. I looked into my little brother's room and decided to place the letter I had written on his bed. Because we never had the relationship I had hoped for, I debated on giving it to him.

I closed the door quietly behind me and looked out at Bo. He looked lost, maybe it was because he didn't know what was wrong with me, or maybe because of something completely unrelated.

I asked him under my breath to take me to Jer's and he agreed but not another word was spoken between us.

I could feel the knots in my stomach starting to multiply, and Bo was feeding off of my tension.

As we pulled up in front of his house, Bo looked at me offering to go in, so I didn't have to go alone.

Without saying anything to him I responded with a small shake of my head. Jer's car wasn't there so I assumed he wasn't home anyway. As I pressed through the door the feeling of home that I once felt had completely dissolved. I ran into the bedroom and saw all of my items already in my bag, and as I reached to grab it I felt someone staring at me. Reluctantly I looked up and saw him standing in the bathroom wearing nothing but his jeans. I immediately closed my eyes hoping that I wasn't walking into what I thought I was.

He just stared, not saying a word. "If I left anything else behind would you mind just shipping it?" I hoped that this would break the ice, or at least give me an easy out.

He looked down and I couldn't read what he was feeling. This was the first time I had ever looked at him like he was a stranger.

"Jer, I can't do this." I tried to keep it together but I could feel the tears coming on.

"Then don't, take your shit and leave." So, I did exactly what he asked me, I grabbed my bag and walked out the door. I thought I heard my name as I closed the door behind me, and then wondered if it was my imagination, or just wishful thinking.

I found enough strength in me to bury my emotions. I put on my poker face and got in the car. Bo slid his hand on my leg, and I nodded giving him the signal to take me home.

Chapter Eighteen

The ride home was a blur. I know I had dozed in and out the whole way. Bo saw me start to open my eyes, and I realized everything that I thought was a nightmare was a reality. I felt emptiness, like I was incomplete.

"So, I know this isn't the best time to ask, but when you said you wanted to go home, did you mean ours or yours?"

I was completely blind-sided, and since I was feeling all out of sorts anyway I decided on the answer that was the easiest, the one that would help me forget.

"Ours." I saw his face immediately light up. "But I swear to God Bo, if you cheat on me." He wouldn't let another word out of my mouth.

"Bells, I wouldn't and I didn't." I could hear the conviction in his voice. And although not an ounce of me believed him I didn't have it in me to fight.

I took another quick look at his beautiful face, and dosed right back into my sound sleep.

Hours could have passed for all I knew when I felt Bo poking me "We are home baby." I slowly opened my eyes and started to grab my bags. It was late and I knew it would be difficult for me to fall back to sleep now.

I pushed past Bo into *our* apartment, wondering when I would be able to actually make this place my home. I saw the Xbox remotes on the couch, the empty beer cans next to the sink, and the trash overflowing.

"Sorry it's a mess, I kind of left in a hurry." I knew from dating Bo for years that this was partially true. Only the trash part though, the rest of it would probably never change. I guess it was time for me to adapt.

"Jane called while you were asleep. She seemed to be trashed, but regardless said she would drive your car back tomorrow."

"Thanks."

I helped myself to a pair of his boxers and he threw me his t-shirt. I know it seems gross, but

I love his smell. He used to leave his undershirts out on the bed for me, and I am glad that he thought to do the same right now. It was comforting to me.

I curled up on the couch and put on TV while he made several trips to bring all of our stuff up. I was flipping through the channels when Pretty Woman was on. I literally clapped my hands together.

"Pretty Woman?" He asked before he could see the tv.

"You know me so well." It was my all-time favorite movie.

"If only I could just be Richard Gere, right?" He looked at me with a half-smile.

"Every princess needs her prince."

He dropped the bags and came over to lay on the couch with me. Sometimes Bo could make me feel like a princess. We finished the movie, and I felt completely relaxed as he ran his fingers through my hair. I found myself drifting fast asleep.

When I woke up it was close to noon. I looked at my phone and had 4 missed calls from Jane, 14 missed calls from Jer, and 3 from my Mom. To top it off I had 4 voicemails from Jer alone. I couldn't decide if I needed to hear them or not. Considering that they were left this morning, I figured he was sober. I decided to listen.

"IZ, CALL ME BACK."

"IZ, I screwed up. I'm sorry, call me back."

"Iz·············.."

I couldn't even listen to the last one. Just hearing his voice made me tear up.

I saw Bo's running shoes missing so I figured he had already gone without me. I needed to run and clear my head. I went to grab my spare pair of shoes when I saw the picture again. I couldn't help but pick it up.

I sat in my bed staring into the picture, and instead of making up another story I just held it. I analyzed every aspect of it. Bo was happy, genuinely happy. She was beautiful and looking up at him. I saw the flowers in the background landscape, and I knew it wasn't taken in the city. I also realized that Bo looked much younger, probably a few years before we even met.

I heard the door open, but I didn't put the picture down. I saw him peek around the corner and I could feel his eyes on me as I laid in his bed and stared at the picture that has always come between us, without either of us realizing it.

"Bells, I need to tell you."

I shook my head, I was finally ready to hear it.

"That woman, her name is Lauren."

"Ok."

"She was my college sweetheart. We were together for 5 years."

"What happened?" I was afraid to know the answer.

"It's a longer story than you want to hear I am sure. So here is the short version. Our Senior year of college she got pregnant."

I held my hand up to my face. I didn't know what to say, or where this was going. Why wasn't he married to her? Why didn't he have the child? And why after being together for five years did I not know this."

"Lauren never told me she was pregnant, she actually broke up with me right before graduation and said that she wanted to make a life for herself, and that didn't include moving to the city with me. She broke my heart."

"I pictured us being married, a future with her."

"What happened to the baby?"

"Well here's the thing, about six months ago I ran into her brother. We were at a bar, and just started talking about where our lives had led us. He accidentally told me that Ella looked just like me. When he realized he screwed up, it was too late. I had already figured it out."

"So⋯.so you have a daughter?"

"Yes, she is beautiful."

"Have you met her?"

"No. Brad, Lauren's brother has been showing me pictures and videos. That's who I was with the night you thought I was cheating on you."

I immediately felt horrible. I always made it about me, and here this whole time he was going through something I couldn't even comprehend.

"I'm Sorry."

"No Bells, I am. I stayed out too late and I did get drunk. It's hard for me to handle talking about her and not being able to be a part of her life."

"So why aren't you?"

"Lauren still doesn't know that I know about her. She broke up with me because she knew I wanted to focus on my career. And honestly, I don't know how to go about being a father to a twelve-year-old girl. Lauren would kill Brad, and I would lose my only lifeline to my daughter."

"So why did you have this picture all these years? You have had it out before you even knew about your daughter."

"Because I thought she was the one that got away. I always had good memories of her, and I wasn't ready to get rid of all of the evidence that what we had was real."

"Bo, that is the sweetest thing I have ever heard you say, even if it wasn't about me."

He let out a loud sigh. "I just···. just needed you to know I wasn't cheating on you. I really do want to take us to the next level."

"Were you ever going to tell me?"

"I was going to tell you when I figured out what I wanted to do about it."

"Well, what do you want to do about it?"

"I'm not sure."

Bo wrapped his arms around me and placed his head on top of mine. Without even realizing it I wiped away his tears, and although I wasn't a fan of emotional men I was completely turned on by his silent tears.

"Bo, I think sometimes we set ourselves up for failure. We are the hardest on ourselves, and we overthink everything. That's why we found each other, and that's why for once you need to let that go. Forgive yourself for not being there, because you didn't even know about her. But now that you do, you need to be a part of that girl's life."

He put his hands on the side of my face and stared into my eyes. It was like he was picturing us together for the rest of our lives, like a switch had been hit and, in that moment, he kissed me, and I knew I was forever his too.

Chapter Nineteen

Six Months Later·········

"Bells have you seen my red tie?"
"No hun, check in the top drawer of the dresser."
I had been editing all the pictures of the last two months and regretting not doing it sooner. Not only had the pictures turned out phenomenal but I would have them done in time for Christmas Cards, but barely.
"Hey." He whispered into my neck, immediately giving me chills.
"Hey to you." I turned and wrapped my legs around him.
"Do you have to go to work?" I placed my hands in between his thighs.
"Ughhhhh Bells don't torment me, you know I'll stay. But then you can't get your work done. And you have a big night with Jane."
I crossed my arms like a five-year-old
"Fine. Have it your way. See you when I get home tonight."
He kissed me softly on my lips "Love you."
"Love you too." As I heard the door close I threw my hair up into a messy bun, took a sip of my tea and glanced over at my phone. I saw the five missed calls from Jane, but knew I couldn't get distracted from my work so I ignored them and moved on.
I had gotten to the last picture that I took. It was beautiful, Ella with her arms wrapped around her father and looking into his eyes. You could feel the emotion through the picture.
Two months after Bo told me about Ella, and after constant nagging from me, he finally reached out to Lauren. Although it took three more months for her to agree to let Ella meet him, it was worth every ounce of anticipation.
Bo and I had grown so much closer as a couple as well. We have been successfully living

together for six months, and neither of us are dead yet, so successful.

It has been exactly 184 days since I have spoken to Jer. Since he doesn't know my new address I have also not received any letters, and since Jane is still at my old apartment she has been given strict orders to throw out any of the letters she gets from him.

As much as I wanted it to work with him, as friends I know that because of our actions on that night I would never be able to go back to being the best friend. Every single emotion I felt for him was real, and raw. I don't think that it was possible for me to look at him without wanting to kiss his lips, or feel his arms wrapped around me.

I remember the first week of living with Bo, at night he would wrap his arms around me and I would silently cry wishing it was Jer. That feeling slowly went away and has been replaced by the love that I felt for Bo. Jane told me I had conditioned my brain to think that it wanted Bo, and whether that was the case or not didn't really matter.

My life was consumed with work, and slowly even my thoughts of Jer disappeared, but I still couldn't help the sick feeling that overwhelmed me when I heard our favorite song. I also learned then when Jer stopped trying to call, I experienced a whole new pain. But with time I learned to ignore that too.

I heard the doorbell ring, and then a twist of the door knob.

"What the hell are you doing in here, not answering my phone calls all morning long?" Jane looked frustrated.

"Sorry lady, I've been finishing these pictures of Bo and Ella. Look how amazing they turned out!"

"I love that you act surprised that they turned out so good, you are dating the hottest guy in New York, and he has the best photographer in the city of course they are going to be fabulous. But I will look anyway just to appease you."

I got up and headed into the kitchen while she was scrolling through the pictures. I heard her take a loud breath in and out. She wasn't trying to hide the dramatics either.

"What Jane?" I thought she had deleted all the pictures.

"Nothing I was just looking at this picture of you and Jer." Ever since I had told Jane about our rendezvous and the reason I am no longer speaking to Jer, anytime we were alone she would try to convince me that we belonged together. She was such a hopeless romantic and I admired that about her, so the first few times I played into it. Telling her that I would go back to him but I just needed time to think. I am pretty sure that we both knew that I wouldn't go back to him, let alone speak to him again.

"You know you still haven't told your mom. She still talks to Jer every other day and acts as if you guys are still the best of friends." I knew that she knew these facts because she also now calls my mother all the time. My mother loved to gossip, and so did Jane. And ever since Jane began driving to my hometown once a month to visit Todd, her and my mother became quite close.

I had figured that night when Jane disappeared that she was hooking up with someone. I don't think that I would have ever guessed it was Todd. Although in hindsight he was her type, hot.

Jane and Todd would take turns visiting each other and Todd has actually become part of our "family" when he was in town. I loved seeing Jane happy, although we both know that neither of them was faithful to each other but right now I think that they were both fine with that.

"So, I know that we were supposed to have girls night tonight but Todd is actually on his way into town. Is there any way we could double date tonight? You know I'd love you forever for it."

"We both know that you would love me forever regardless, but I will ask Bo, I am sure we can."

Jane left the apartment, and went shopping to buy a new outfit for Todd. Every time she went home or he came up it was an excuse for her to shop. I am fairly certain that he has never seen her in the same outfit twice. I guess when you only get to see each other once a month it really counts.

I am pretty sure that Bo sees me in the same pair of three sweats every night. He hasn't complained yet, but that is probably because underneath those very large baggy sweatpants, is a lace bra and matching panties.

As predicted Bo was fine with going out tonight, and I laid our outfits out on the bed. I sat back at the computer and organized our "family" Christmas card. Since most of our friends knew about Ella, I suggested that we use one with her in it this year. Bo always seemed so appreciative that I welcomed her with open arms. Although it's hard not to, she is an amazing little girl and she has her Daddy's smile.

We have only seen her six times since they first met, and each time we both loved her more and more. Last time Lauren even let her spend the night with us.

I have never felt so insecure about myself than when I first met Lauren. Bo told her that I would be coming when Ella first met Bo in central park. Lauren had driven from Connecticut early in the morning to meet us, which Bo thanked her a hundred times for.

Bo and I were sitting on the bench, his leg shaking nervously. "What if she hates me?" "Bo are you serious? It is impossible to hate you?"

I knew the second I saw her, that she was Bo's. I even thought to myself that I would have pointed that fact out if she were a stranger on the street. Lauren was holding her hand, and I was immediately taken back by how beautiful she was. It would have been a miracle for Bo and Lauren to have an average looking child.

Lauren had long dark hair, and a petite figure. She was dressed as if she had walked out of a J Crew magazine, and her friendly personality radiated. The picture that Bo kept of her didn't do her any justice.

Before I had met her, I was so nervous about many things. First, I was nervous that Bo would immediately leave me and fall back in love with her all over again. Then I was nervous that she would hate me, and try to keep me away from Ella. But Lauren was none of those things, I could never hate her, in fact I actually grew to love her.

We talk about once a week on the phone, and normally skype twice a week with Ella. We all had such a strange relationship, but it worked and I could tell that a void that I didn't even know existed in Bo was filled.

"Bells, have you been sitting here all day?" I jumped in my seat.

"Sorry, I just zoned out I guess. And no, I haven't been sitting here all day, I've done the dishes, went for a run, edited the pictures, picked out your outfit and ironed, which I deserve extra points for because you know I hate it."

"Ok, Cindy." After the first week of living together Bo ever so kindly nicknamed me Cindy short for Cinderella, because he said I acted like a slave when I had to clean.

"Hey Cindy, I'm hoping in the shower if you care to join···."

And on that note Bo and I took a very long, hot steamy shower together before getting ready for the evening.

Chapter Twenty

"AHHHHHHHH You're finally here!" Jane wrapped her arms around me as if we hadn't seen each other in years. Which gave away the fact that she was probably already wasted.

"Hey guys, good to see you." Todd shook Bo's hand firmly. He bent down and kissed my hand, and I thought I saw Bo clench his teeth. I could also tell that Todd was well on his way to being hammered.

Bo leaned over and whispered in my ear "So maybe we should have pre-gamed?" I let out an obnoxiously loud laugh. "It wasn't that funny."

"No, it wasn't but Jane on the dance floor right now is."

We all turned to look in her direction as she was doing her best to do "the sprinkler"

Todd went out and joined her. "Well maybe they are perfect for each other." Bo and I found a table in the corner and waited for their return.

"You know you really are something." I felt Bo's fingers down the side of my arm. "And why is that?" I asked, leaning in close to him.

"Because you made me fight, when I wanted to surrender. You filled my life with a love I didn't even know I wanted. You made me whole, when I didn't even know I was broken."

Without another word I pressed my body into his, forgetting that we were in a public place I kissed him like it was the first time. I felt his hands on my neck and then I felt another pair of hands pulling him away from me.

"What the hell?" I opened my eyes to see my little brother standing there, with Jer right behind him.

"Iz, we need you to come back to the apartment with us, Now." I felt my knees weak, I stood but then fell straight to the floor. I completely blacked out and woke up in my apartment. As in Jane's apartment.

"Where is Bo?" I demanded.

Red looked at me nervously. "He's uh downstairs waiting."

"Waiting for what? What the hell is going on Red? Are mom and Dad ok?" I started crying. I knew whatever it was it couldn't be good if they were both here.

"Just calm down Iz." Jer put his arms around me. I immediately felt calm, but I didn't want to. "Get off me Jer."

"Ok Ok I get it." He backed up slowly and put his hands down.

I looked over and Red was crying. "Ok someone needs to tell me what the hell is going on NOW!"

Jer stood up and walked closer to me. "Um, I didn't know where else to take him. I mean he came to me for advice, and my advice was to come to you." He paused and looked over at Red.

"Jess is pregnant." My little brother started crying out loud now.

I didn't know what to do so I looked at Jer and walked over to put my arms around my brother.

"I need you to come home with me to tell mom and dad."

"Oh no you don't Jer, I wasn't the one to have sex with her." I felt his arms squeeze around me, and I couldn't remember the last time we had actually hugged each other.

"I know, I just didn't know what to do. I went to Jer's and he put me in the car and drove me here."

I glanced over at Jer and mouthed *thank you*, I then realized how incredibly sexy he looked. He had a punisher t-shirt on and his arms were covered in tattoos, many more than the last time that I saw him. His blue eyes were piercing and his dark hair was much shorter than the last time I saw him. I felt chills down my spine, and closed my eyes to block everything out.

"Ok Red, just call down. Listen to me, everything will work out. I promise you, and we are going to love this baby so much. You have to be the one to tell mom and dad, I will go with you, but only as support."

"That's it? You aren't going to lecture me about getting my life together?"

"Oh trust me we have a 13 hour drive ahead of us for that."

He hugged me again. And didn't have to say a word.

"I need to go to my apartment and pack."

"So, you really live with him?" Jer asked and probably didn't mean to say it out loud.

"Yes. I do, I am in love with him." I could see Jer flinch.

Right on queue Bo walked in. "Hey Baby, everything ok?"

"Yeah, but I am going to need to go home for a few days. Jess is pregnant."

Bo's face fell. I couldn't tell if he was feeling sorry for Red or if he was afraid for me to go back home with Jer.

Bo leaned into Red "You were right to come to your sister, she is amazing." I noticed that Jer snuck out when Bo came in. I almost wanted to pay for us to all fly back home to avoid the awkward conversations on the way back.

In the cab on the way home Bo was rubbing my hand and his leg was shaking. "Bo you don't have to worry, I'll be back in a few days."

"You never told me what happened between you two." Bo was right, ever since we got home I avoided it at all costs. I told him we had a disagreement, and we had outgrown each other. I felt a pang of guilt, realizing that for the past six months Bo probably thought that he was the reason I had cut Jer off. He probably thought I chose him over Jer. If things had gone differently that night, it may have been the opposite.

"We just didn't see things the same anymore." I felt my whole body tighten up.

"Should I be worried about you driving home with him? Do you need me to go with you?"

"No, I'm fine. I need to be there for Red. I'll be back in a few days I promise."

"Ok, I'll help you pack. Hopefully I can keep the apartment halfway decent while you're gone."

"You better because if I come home to an apartment filled with empty beer cans, Xbox, and six other grown men acting like children you'll be in trouble." I laughed. Once a month Bo still had guys' night, but instead of going out they started staying in, I would make snacks and they would play video games all night long. It made me appreciate not dating any boys in a fraternity. But it also made me appreciate the ability men have to just let everything go.

I feel like when Jane and I get together for girl's night, we still vent about everything that has bothered us in the last week. It's hard for us to just put everything out of our minds the way that men seem to do. For that I am envious.

I stared out of the cab's window into the night. I hadn't even realized where Jane and Todd ended up. "Where⋯" I didn't get the sentence out before Bo finished it. "They're at our place. She is packing your things."

"Did she already know?"
"No but she said Jer called her an hour before we got to the club to find out where we would be. I called her to tell her why they were here, and she headed over to pack your things."

"She's the best." I sighed. "My appointments"
"I'll have them all rescheduled. Please for once let me be there for you. Let me take care of everything for you. Just go and be there for him. I'll be here for you."

God he was amazing. I can't even believe how far we have come. I pressed my back into his chest and let myself synchronize our breathing. "I am so lucky."
"Ah Bells, you know that I am the lucky one." He pressed his lips to my forehead, and I melted into him.

"We're here." I must have dozed off. I really hope that Jane had everything already packed, I wouldn't even know what to bring right now. I probably would throw a bunch of random items together and just hope it worked out.

I knew that it wouldn't take Jer long to get here from the other apartment, they were practically right behind us. I felt kind of bad that they didn't want to stay considering they had just made that long drive.

I am sure that my brother just wanted to get it over with. I was really happy that even though Jer wasn't a part of my life anymore, that he had stayed a part of Reds. Honestly Red was probably closer with him than he was with me. I was ok with that; especially because I was never home to be there for him.

I walked into the apartment, and Jane came running for me. Oh shit, she was definitely drunk which made me reconsider my request for her to pack my stuff for me.

"Auntie B!" I was right, and now I was glad that I was leaving. Todd just shrugged his shoulders. "He Bo, can I get you something to drink? You're probably going to need it."

"Sure, get me the strongest I have in the fridge." The boys sat down on the couch and Jane was pulling me into my room.

"Ok. So, I have almost everything packed, I think you just need a bathing suit or two." She was throwing clothes everywhere, and I was having a small anxiety attack.

"Jane it is 40 degrees outside. I don't need a bathing suit."

"Jer has a hot tub." She winked at me and was thrusting her hips. I mouthed stop it. I think she took the hint and she pulled her fingers up to her lips as if she was sealing them shut…if only that truly worked.

I heard the door open and I knew that Jer was here to take me back home. I got knots in my stomach and felt light headed, consumed by my anxiety. Jane came over and whispered, "Is it just me or did he get really hot?" Ugh…."I think he got hotter." I said, I hate to admit it to myself.

I walked into the living room and saw that Todd had just poured three shots, I walked up without caring, or thinking and downed all of them.

"Seriously?" Todd huffed.

"There's plenty more bartenders. I needed some liquid courage."

"Point taken. Have a safe trip." He put out his hand for a high five, I laughed as Jane ran in and intercepted it.

Bo picked up my bag and followed Jer out to the car. As I walked down the steps I saw Bo almost looking angry whispering something into Jer's ear. Then he walked over to me and gave me a very long, delicious, kiss. I was sure to mark his territory. "Be safe. Call me when you get there. I love you." He said the last part extra loud.

Jer slammed his door shut. I saw Red asleep in the back seat, so I jumped in the front and sat in silence for the first half an hour on this long journey.

J. Desails

Chapter Twenty-One

"Are you going to say anything this whole trip?"
Jer finally broke the ice.
"What do you want me to say Jer?"
"I don't know anything I guess."
I was feeling irritated and also a little buzzed. "Fine
Jer, you broke my fucking heart. I loved you, I
wanted you to want me to stay, beg me to stay,
fight for me. But you didn't so I gave up on
everything."
"Loved." He whispered.
"What?'
"you said you loved me···as in past tense."
"Yes, that's right Jer, past tense."
I saw him peering into the back seat to make sure
Red was still asleep. He lowered his voice again.
"I am so sorry Iz." I turned to face the window and
drifted fast asleep.

     I woke up about thirty minutes prior to the
North Carolina line, but I decided to pretend to
sleep, to be nosy of course. I hear Red talking to
Jer about how excited he really was to be a father.
How he would give up all his hopes and dreams to
make his child's come true. I cried tears of joy, and
tears of pain for my brother.

     I was so happy that he would get to
experience a family of his own, but my heart broke
knowing that he was right, there were so many
dreams of his that would never come true. I also
felt Jessica's pain. I knew that she would also be
giving up so much.

     I thought about Red's dreams of going into
the military, and how that probably would never
happen. I remembered driving him to Camp
Lejeune right after I got my license so that he
could see the osprey's flying. I also remember Jer
having the same dream, yet look at where he is
now. So I guess baby or not, some dreams take a
back burner to life.

     I felt so fortunate that I was able to make
mine come true, but there were aspects of my life
that I would trade in a heartbeat for the career. I

looked at Jer, and wished that he would have known I would have given everything up for him.

"Hey Iz, you're up." He nudged my shoulder.

"We are getting ready to stop for some grub, you came?" Red was practically in the front seat.

"I'm always game for fast food, even if my body isn't."

After fighting for an hour over where we would go to eat, we ended up at a small diner. I didn't say much, but I watched and took in everything. I smiled because I wanted to pretend that everything was fine between Jer and I.

I wanted to go back to the laughing, and bickering that all existed in the years before I let our friendship dwindle away. When Red got up to go to the bathroom, Jer slid into the seat beside me.

"Are you going to tell me who she is?" I could feel his breath on my shoulder.

"Who?" I had no idea where this conversation was coming from. "The little girl, the one in your pictures. Who is she?"

I felt a pang of guilt for leaving the city, knowing that Ella would be staying the weekend. "She is Bo's daughter." I saw his face drop. I thought that he would have put the clues together by the picture, unless he saw only the one where I was holding her hand. Bo had taken that picture, and without any editing whatsoever it became the background on my laptop.

"You've always wanted a little girl." He said it as if Bo had handed me the world. I had never verbalized my want or desire to have children. I had always been so consumed with my career that I just didn't have time for it. But I knew that Jer would catch me staring at a family, even amidst my busiest days on the job when he would come visit me. It was probably a dead giveaway when I would email him all the photos I had edited of families and put in the subject line *best shoot ever.*

I inhaled a deep breath and told him about Lauren withholding Ella from Bo for twelve years. I think saying it out loud made me feel so happy that

Jess decided to involve my brother, and give him a choice to make. I know that deep down Lauren was probably afraid of rejection, so she shielded herself from it. I couldn't blame her for that part, but I could never fully forgive her for stealing that choice away from Bo.

I knew that second that Bo looked into Ella's eyes that a new pain had formed, and although it was buried by the happiness Ella fulfilled, it would always be there. I looked over at Jer, and I could tell that he saw the pain in my eyes and she wasn't even my child.

"Thank you." He said standing, to allow Red to sit back down. I knew that he was thanking me for letting him in a little bit. I'm sure at this point he would take anything. I know this because as badly as it hurt cutting him off, I'd always wanted him to fight for our friendship, just a little longer, and a little harder.

Jer paid the bill and we hopped back into the car for the rest of the drive. We actually ended up singing our hearts out to 90's on 9 radio. That made the time fly and before I knew it we were right outside of our hometown. I could tell because Red stopped singing, and I saw his forehead beaded with sweat from the rearview mirror.

"Red, has there ever been a time that you thought they wouldn't love you?"
"What do you mean?" His voice was even shaky.
" I mean have you ever thought that mom and dad would give up on you? Like when they caught you smoking pot, or when you wrecked your first car or when you got suspended for fighting at school?"

"No." he grabbed my shoulder. "See this is why I made Jer come get you."
"I thought it was Jer's idea."
"It was, but I'm going to take credit for it because it was so great."

We all laughed and I hoped that was enough to loosen him up before he told our parents. I told him that I would be in the room, but I wasn't going to say a word. I felt like it was his battle, and Lord knows although I convinced him otherwise, I was so glad to not be in his position right now.

I was also surprised that Jer hadn't stepped in and said anything. I know that he had heavy opinions on this matter, considering he was born when his parents were just eighteen. They had to make the same decisions that Red was faced with and I was sure glad they made the right one.

"Well we are five minutes out. I am going to drop you guys off around the corner, don't want to be caught as the accomplice." He laughed.

"You will drop us off right out front, and you will be our getaway car." I nudged him in the side. He smiled at me, and I knew that he was thinking we were back on the right path. I didn't want to crush him and let him know that I wasn't even sure how to get back there.

As we pulled up to the house I saw my nosy mother peeking out the window, and throwing her hand over her face running towards the car. Maybe I was just the distraction Red was hoping for, and suddenly I felt like a pawn in this game.

Before I could get unbuckled my mother was trying to pry me out of the car.

"What's wrong, what happened, why are you here? Are you pregnant?" Well I promised him I wouldn't say anything, but I thought what the hell let's see where it goes.

"I'm not but Red has something to tell you." I pointed to him.

He threw his hand up over his face to shield himself, probably with good reason.

"Jess is pregnant." My mother without even thinking reached into the back of the car and grabbed him by the ear.

I backed up and heard mumbles of his full name, followed by tears, some smacking and then finally a hug. I sat on the porch watching this amazing woman love her child that probably told her the hardest thing he would ever say. I wanted to be a mother like that one day. I felt an arm slip around my shoulder, and before I could shove him off I looked over to see my father.

"Did he finally tell her that Jess is pregnant?" I stared at him with my mouth completely open.

"You knew! I drove 13 hours to be here for support and you knew!"

"Well in his defense, he didn't know that I knew. But I am pretty sure your mom had an idea too. Jess has been requesting pies from your mother every other day, and complaining of nausea." He pulled me in tighter.

"Are you mad?"

"No, I am proud that he is being a man about it, although now that I know he ran to his sister for help I'm not so sure I should give him all the credit for having the balls."

"I'm glad he came to me Dad, it's the first time he has ever come to me for anything. I was just thinking at his graduation how we really didn't have a relationship. How I wanted so badly for him to need me. I didn't necessarily want it to be for this reason, but I am happy for him."

"Baby girl, there comes a time in everyone's life where we come back to family. We don't think we ever need them so they sit in the back of our minds, but the second that we need something, whether it be comfort from fear, or even to share happiness they are the first ones we share it with."

I smiled and looked over to Jer. He was my family; how could I have just let him slip away so easily.

Chapter Twenty-Two

Mom insisted that everyone stay for dinner. She always cooks when she is worried, lucky for Jess.

I still hadn't said much to Jer, he came and sat next to me in the living room and whispered into my ear "Come stay the night with me, I need to tell you something."

Without even thinking I shook my head. Why had I just agreed to this? I had no idea what he needed to say to me, but I felt like I owed it to him to at least listen.
I spent the rest of the evening showing my Mom some of the pictures I had saved on my phone of Ella; my mother was much less forgiving of Lauren than I was.

She asked me when I thought Bo and I would get married, right in front of Jer making the entire situation ten times more awkward than it already was. I guess she just assumed that I still informed him of everything. I failed to mention that I had overheard him on the phone with my father a week ago asking him for his permission.

I looked over at Jer and saw his face was rigid. He was trying his hardest to show no emotion but I saw right through it all. I wondered if he was inviting me over to tell me something about Melissa, maybe that he was also planning on marrying her. I assumed they were still together, but it just dawned on me that I also never asked.

Well I guess I technically can't say that I forgot, I had been wanting to ask him since the second I saw him in the club, but my heart wasn't ready to hear the answer.

I was helping Mama clean up the dishes in the kitchen and told her I would be staying over with Jer tonight. "Well just behave yourself, you're about to be a married woman···whoops let it slip." I guess if I wasn't as nosy as her I would have been surprised by that "accidental" slip up.

"I've got it under control mom, it's just Jer."

"Right. That's why I am concerned. Well I will see you first thing in the morning." She said it as if I was fifteen years old again and had a curfew.

I hugged everyone goodbye, including Red who was now accompanied by Jess. Figures she shows up after the dirty work has been done.

I went to get in the car and Jer opened the door for me. I didn't say a word, because I honestly had no idea where to start. I had just planned on letting him spill his news and get on with our lives.

As soon as we pulled up to his house he turned to me. "Are you going to marry him?"

"That's not what you asked me here for is it?"

"No."

"Then I am not giving you that answer."

I grabbed my bag and walked right into his house, declaring that I was sleeping in the bed tonight, by myself. He put his hands up in surrender. He knew after last time he didn't even have a shot winning this battle.

I felt him coming up behind me and without turning around I told him "Jer I have not had a shower, whatever it is you need to tell me I have a feeling I am going to need comfy clothes and no make-up."

"You're probably right." He turned and left the room.

I took my bag into his bathroom and felt overwhelmed with emotion. I laid out my clothes and undressed, pausing before I reached the shower. I stared into the steaming water as if the night we had was painted on the walls. I had to place my hands on the wall, when I heard his voice. "Just breathe." I saw that the door was shut, and I knew that he was sitting on the other side. I felt the wave of tears streaming down my face and I slowly took a deep breath and got in the shower. I rubbed my hand over the tattoo on my side, and said it out loud, slowly *just breathe.*

I knew he had no idea about the tattoo, I got it three weeks after we stopped talking, and convinced myself it was the only way for me to get through each day. Bo loved it and didn't ask any questions about the reasoning behind it. I closed my eyes and tried to shut out the memories that were flooding me.

Finally, after what seemed like an hour, and possibly could have been since the water was now cold I had gained enough strength to face whatever he needed to tell me on the other side of the door.

I looked at my phone and saw a text from Bo, I opened it and saw a picture of him and Ella *miss you!* I quickly typed a response and my heart felt heavy, and guilty. I knew it would crush Bo if he were aware of where I was, even though he didn't know the whole story of what happened here.

I pulled myself together, put on my big girl pants, well sweat pants and slowly opened the door. I saw Jer next to the bed taking his watch off and sliding it into the drawer. My eyes were fixated on his amazing body, was it even possible that he could look better than he had six months ago? I noticed that his sleeve was completed, and his abs couldn't possibly be more chiseled. He let out a half smile and I could see the gap between his teeth. He was always so self-conscious about it, as if everyone in the world stared at it. Little did he know, no one else noticed except for me.

My eyes made it to his. He stared right into me, and I wanted to forgive him for everything that happened. My heart almost forgot everything that he said. His phone rang, pulling me back into reality.

"I have to take this, I'll be right back." I nodded and jumped in the bed. I began texting Jane, when he stepped back into the room.

"May I?" He looked next to me, asking permission to get in the bed with me.
"On the outside of the covers." He let out a chuckle and slid on the bed.
"What is it Jer?"
"Melissa and I broke up." *Seriously?* This is why I am sleeping in his bed tonight.
"I'm sorry?" I knew he could tell how confused I looked.

"I just wanted you to know that she wasn't the one."

I laid further into the bed, not knowing which direction this conversation was going in, or where I wanted it to go for that matter. I was with Bo now, I was content, I was over Jer. Or was I? He still had no shirt on and was only wearing jeans, I wanted so badly to reach over and place my hand on his stomach, or lay my head on his chest.

After another minute of neither of us saying anything, I saw he was getting frustrated and got up and walked to the porch. I heard the door slam shut and against my mind's better judgment I jumped out of bed and followed him.

"What the hell?" I threw my hands up in the air. "Why in the hell did you bring me all the way over here to tell me that she wasn't the one? I already knew that!"

"Did you? Did you really already know that? You have no idea what is going on in my life, your mom said you never ask about me, Jane says you've sworn her to secrecy. For all you know I could have been married with a kid on the way by now."

I could tell he was getting frustrated. "Just breathe Jer." I placed my hand on his chest and he put his hand over top mine. I pressed my forehead into his chest, and felt his lips on my shoulder.

"Why aren't you with her? Why isn't she the one?" I wanted honesty now more than ever. "Because it's you and it always has been." He let out a deep breath that I knew he had been holding in for far too long.

I looked up at him, the man that helped me become who I am, and the man I had loved for years. Without thinking about Bo, or Ella, or myself for that matter I pressed my lips firmly to his.

I felt his hands wrap around me, and I felt his tongue graze my lips. I gently bit his bottom lip and pressed my hand on his stomach.

"You can't do that Iz, I won't be able to stop."
"I wasn't planning on stopping you."

Jer picked me up and I wrapped my legs around him. He was walking us towards the bedroom; I pushed every logical thought from my mind. I've waited my whole life to be with this man, whether I knew it or not.

He gently laid me onto the bed, and kissed my forehead. He started pulling my shirt up and looked at me for approval. I nodded my head and started shaking with anticipation, as his hands brushed over my nipples. He pressed his lips into mine once again, and I knew I never wanted to leave this moment.

"Iz, are you sure?" I nodded slowly.

I felt him pull my sweatpants off and throw them to the floor. "You are···. amazing." He paused and kissed my cheek. "I love you." "I love you too Jer." Are you sure you're ready?"

"Yes. I've been waiting for this moment forever." With that I felt Jer slowly enter me for the first time. He was nothing short of amazing, and I felt years of emotions and passion pouring out.

I grabbed the sheets around us, and watched him as his mouth moved all over my entire body. It was like he wanted to be personal with every inch of me, but simultaneously stay inside of me. I've been with other men before, but he felt like my first. It felt like everything was starting to make sense.

I pulled his face into mine and started at him, his ice blue eyes as he was thrusting in and out of me. I felt it more with every entry. "Slow down." I could barely speak the words.

"Why baby?" he whispered as he bit my earlobe gently. "I'm going to···." Too late. I felt him move faster and saw that he was on his way too. I looked up at him as he bit his own lip and closed his eyes. He let out a small groan, and it filled me with satisfaction.

The next morning, I woke up to his gorgeous face and the sunlight sneaking in through the blinds. I started studying all of the tattoos he had acquired in the months we had been apart. I traced them on his arm, and I stopped when I came across the one on his side, in almost the identical spot as mine *just breathe.*

"Hey you." He threw his arms around me.

"You know it's true what they say, great minds think alike."

"Oh, and why is that my love?" I got butterflies the moment he called me my love.

I turned and raised my arm exposing my tattoo. He put his hand on it, almost in disbelief. "Really?" I leaned over and kissed him again. "I don't think I could ever get sick of kissing you."

"I don't think I ever want you to get sick of kissing me."

"Jer, why did you act like that before I left? You were so···so hateful."

"Um, Iz about that. I haven't really told you all of the story."

Just as I thought he was about to put all those broken pieces back together that I left on the floor here six months ago, my brother walked in.

"Izabella???" I pressed a quick kiss to his lips, and knew I was going to have to be patient. "In here." I let out an annoyed huff.

"Oh great, well Mom sent me over to get you, apparently she has a ton planned for the two of you today, and thank God you are here to keep all the focus off of me." I threw a pillow at him, of course she sent him over to get me.

"Alright give me a few minutes to get my shit together." He walked out into the living room and I ran my hand over my tattoo one more time, as I peeked into the bathroom, and watched as Jer brushed his teeth. He was wearing nothing but a towel and I was tempted to go in and hide there for the rest of the day.

I knew it wouldn't take long for my mother to find me, so instead I just told him I would catch up with him later today. He tried to tell me something through the brushing, but hearing my little brother calling my name, I knew I didn't have much time before he came back in.

Chapter Twenty-Three

My Mother was going on and on about how she is giving him two months to get his shit together before she steps in. I don't blame her, and I think it's great parenting to let him fret a little bit about what he was going to do to support his family.

Jess started waiting tables, and I knew Red had given up his hopes on College. I just didn't know what he was going to do in the meantime to support her. Mom told me that he assured her he had something figured out, but wasn't ready to share his master plan just yet.

"So how was it over there last night?" She asked and winked at me. Which made things awkward, and confusing. "Nothing happened, we just talked." I felt my cheeks getting red and I knew that she could tell. Thankfully she didn't press the issue any.

"You know I'm not stupid. I know that you guys haven't spoken since you left here." I knew that she was too good to miss that one.

"Oh really? And how is it that you are so sure."

"Because I know you would have called me when you found out."

"Found out what Mother?" And this is where I knew my Mom all too well, if she did know something she wasn't about to hand it over to me. So as predicted she changed the subject, and we wound up at Babies r Us.

I knew that she was always passive aggressive, but I didn't realize how much so until today. Well I knew that I wanted to hear whatever it was from Jer anyway so I decided just to wait it out. I mean how bad could it be? I didn't see a wife and kid at his house last night.

Mom asked me if I had brought clothes for tonight, we were going to a celebration at Unc's. I am sure that Jane put something halfway decent inside, and I know even if she didn't I would have to drive at least an hour away to find something acceptable.

I assumed that it was a celebration for Red and Jess, considering how my Mom was suddenly over the moon about becoming a grandma.

We were back at the house and I was getting ready when Bo called. I was actually surprised that this was the first time he had called today. Without hesitation I answered.

We didn't say much, and I got to talk to Ella for a few minutes. He asked when I was coming home and I promised by the end of the week. He told me that he had my entire schedule rearranged but I would have to be back on Monday. I told him I loved him, because I was sure that I did. I just wasn't sure if it would ever be enough.

"Are you ready?" Mom peeked her head in the door. All I had that was halfway decent was a plain button down, and a pair of skinny jeans, so I just made it work. She could tell I was a little frustrated with my outfit selection. "It's just Uncs. You have five minutes to meet us out front."

I threw on some blush and nude lip-gloss, and started for the door. When we pulled up I saw Jer's truck out back and instantly got excited. Mom and Dad walked in and I tried to peak my head out back to see if he was outside. He wasn't, but Melissa was.

Any color I had left on my skin vanished. I felt like I was going to be sick, and had déjà vu from six months ago. I couldn't believe that I fell for his shit again. She disappeared into the bar, and as badly as I wanted to cry, to break down and just leave the old Jer wouldn't have let me.

I stepped into the bar and saw a huge Welcome Home sign. I was so confused and looked around to see any faces that I would have recognized from the past. I saw Jer by the bar he got up and ran over to me throwing his arms around me and pressing his lips to mine.

"Hey Baby. What are you doing here?" I still wasn't sure why I was here. But I was momentarily pleased that I was when I took note that Melissa had witnessed the kiss Jer just planted on me.

"Um Mom brought me, I thought it was a celebration for Red and Jess." I saw a look of worry on his face. "You mean she didn't tell you why she brought you?"

"Obviously not Jer, care to fill me in." Before he could open his mouth three guys came in the door and started yelling his name.

I heard muffles of it's been forever, how are you holding up, do you love it. I looked at him and tilted my head to the side. I saw the chain around his neck and felt a lump in my throat. He looked over at me, and I turned to get some air.

I knew he saw me take off, and I was pretty sure that he knew I figured it out.

I was hyperventilating, *how could he*. I felt my knees begin to give out so I went to the side of the bar and bent down.

"Iz, baby. I'm sorry I've been trying to tell you."

"How long?" He put his arms around me, which was pretty ballsy on his part. "I left for basic a week after you left here."

I looked directly into his eyes because for this next part I wanted to be sure he was telling me the truth. "How long before that did you sign your contract?"

"uh…um three months."

"Are you fucking kidding me Jer? You've had 9 fucking months to tell me this, we were best friends, I told you everything."

"Iz, I tried to tell you when I came to New York, then the whole Bo thing happened."

"Is that why you really broke up with Melissa? Because you were leaving?"

"No Melissa knew everything, she knew that I was using her to push you away because I was afraid you would hate me for not telling you. She knew that up until the day I left she was just a distraction."

"Did everyone know except me?"

I could tell he didn't want to answer this question. So, he avoided it all together.

"I thought you would be happy for me, you always told me I should live my life with no regrets! So I finally grew enough balls to do it, and you're acting like this!"

"Do not, do not put this on me. This was all you, and I am not mad at your decision to do something you love, I am mad at the decision you made every single day to wake up and not tell me."

I got up and snatched the keys out of his hands. I just needed to be alone. I jumped into his truck and headed for the pier.

It felt like it took me hours to get there, and I was surprised that I hadn't cried at all. I wanted it so bad, but I wasn't sure why. Should I cry because he really did love me, he wasn't ever really going to marry Melissa? Or should I cry because my best friend kept such a huge secret from me for so long.

I shoved the car in park and ran into the sand, like if my feet didn't hit it in ten seconds it would disappear. I sat on the beach for what felt like hours. I left my phone in the car, and never wore a watch so I really had no clue how long it had been.

I closed my eyes and just listened to the waves, the sound of silence that I never could get enough of. "Hey." He came up and sat behind me, with his legs on each side.

"I'm sorry. I could sit here and give you all of the excuses I've made to not tell you, but that's all they are⋯ excuses."

He still hadn't seen my face, and I was sure that he thought I had been crying since I left the bar. I almost wanted to show him, he would be so proud.

"Do you love me?" I said it in a whisper. "More than life itself. The thing is if I hadn't ruined things with us before you left, you would be dealing of a whole other grief when you found out that I was leaving."

"That's an excuse Jer."

"I know, and you don't deserve any more of them. So here goes⋯" He leaned into my neck and started whispering in my ear, his voice was deep and raspy and I had chills all over my body.

"I have wanted you my entire life. I have loved you for my entire life. I can't even stand that I hurt you, and I don't know what my game plan was. I honestly didn't know if I would ever tell you, and don't be mad at your family I swore them to secrecy. I assured them it would crush you, so they would stay quiet."

"Did Jane know?"

"Hell no, I knew she couldn't keep that a secret."

"So, what now?"

"That's your call to make. I am getting stationed in Virginia, I have to leave next week."

"I⋯ I don't know if I can." We both knew the unspoken question that I was answering.

"I know, I'm not asking you to. I am just telling you that no matter where I am in the world, or what I am doing it will always be you."

I finally turned to face him and pressed him into the sand. I threw my shirt off and pulled his over his head. Jer didn't say another word for the rest of the night, because I didn't give him an opportunity to open it. That night I had the best sex of my life, on the beach, with my best friend. I woke up in his bed, and looked over to see him soundly sleeping next to me. I felt a little guilty for making him miss his own welcome home party. He looked so peaceful so I decided to let him sleep.

I threw on one of his oversized t shirts, that still smelled like him. I made some tea and went to sit on his porch. I saw the steam coming up from the water, much like the steam coming from my drink. I had no idea what this day was going to bring. I had no idea what I wanted. That isn't completely true, I knew I wanted Jer I just didn't know if I could handle everything that came with him now.

I needed to go home, I needed to think. And with that, I booked the first flight back to New York.

Chapter Twenty-Four

As I sat on the plane I thought, maybe
running again wasn't the best idea. I figured by
now Jer was probably reading the letter that I
wrote him, and I wanted so badly to be there to
comfort him.

Hey you,

*I can't even begin to say how sorry I
am that I am even writing this letter, because it
means I have already left. This weekend has been
nothing short of amazing with you. For the first
time in my life I felt like I was exactly where I
needed to be, until I found out about where you had
really been.*

*I wish that we could have worked it out, and
I wish that I was strong enough to fight for you, but
after the past six months my strength has been
depleted. I can't even tell you that I am mad,
because I'm not. I am so proud of the choices you
made, and I started wondering if I were in your
position could I have done the same? I wish you the
best in life. This isn't goodbye.*

*See you when I see
you,*

Iz

p.s. I always knew Clark Kent was under there⋯⋯

Before I decided I had made the wrong
decision, I plugged in my earphones and fell fast
asleep until I landed in the city.

"Bells! God, I missed you." Bo lifted me off
of my feet and I felt a pang of guilt right in the pit
of my stomach. I still hadn't decided if I would tell
him what happened between Jer and I. When he
looked at me I felt as if the tables had turned, and I
was running to him instead of Jer for help.

"I missed you too! What's on the agenda for
today?" I needed something to get my mind off of
everything.

"Well, first of all you have a lunch date with Jane, I'm so glad she will be back to pestering you."

"Is Todd still here?"

"Yes, and neither of them have left the apartment since you left."

I thought that was a little weird, trouble in paradise maybe? Typically, Jane couldn't wait to get back to her apartment to do God knows what to him. Well I may have to spill my guts about this weekend after all, but knowing her I am sure I would have plenty of time before I even got a chance to open my mouth.

"Before you go in I have a surprise for you."

"Ok well where is it?"

"She⋯.is right here."

Ella ran out and threw her arms around me. I thought for sure she had already gone back to Connecticut.

"What are you doing here Ella Bella?" I smiled down at her, thrilled that I got to spend some time with her.

"Mom is letting me stay for the whole week! Can you take me shopping?"

"Of course, I can't wait, this is the best surprise ever!"

Bo looked over at us, and it felt right. I was sad that I would even have to leave her for a few hours to have lunch with Jane.

I walked into the apartment and saw Todd on the couch playing video games, and Jane in my kitchen cooking. This was bad. Jane never cooks, and I was pretty sure she didn't even know how.

"The place isn't on fire, so I guess that's a good thing." I wrapped my arms around her, as she turned around I saw her eyes glassy. "What's wrong?" she mouthed to me to be quiet and put her finger over her lips.

Ok, Ok. I never see Jane like this, so without even thinking I grabbed her arm, and announced that we had to go, and directed Bo to finish whatever she was cooking.

We got two blocks away when I broke the silence "What is wrong?"

"I just don't know anymore." Ok, she was having a breakdown. "Start from the beginning."

We made it into a small café and she unloaded everything on me. I felt like a horrible friend because for the past year, it has always been about me. Probably because I just thought she always had it under control.

Apparently, I was right about her and Todd, neither had been faithful to each other. She told me when they started hooking up, it was nothing more than just some company and good sex. But then Jane fell. Hard. She told me the last time she went to visit him something just clicked and she wanted to be with him, like really be with him. She even said she would move to the country with him.

"Have you told him any of this?"

"No, and I just can't. I want him to say it to me first."

"Trust me Jane, with Todd you may be waiting a very long time for that."

"I know. I know. I just don't know what to do anymore."

"I think we need a vacation."

"Stop it, don't play with me."

"I'm serious Jane. Clear your schedule next week; I'll book us a flight to the keys. Just me and you."

I was glad that she went for it, because I didn't know what advice to give her right now. I didn't want Todd to break her heart and I wasn't ready for her to move away from me either. I know the last part is selfish, but I can't even help it.

I couldn't even remember the last time I had gone on vacation. I know Bo would be a little disappointed, but I know he would also understand that I needed it. I looked at my phone for the hundredth time today and still no call or messages from Jer.

I tried to hide my disappointment but I know it was written all over my face.

"He will come for you. I promise." I hadn't even told her about me sleeping with him. I couldn't even think about being with Bo after that, it wouldn't even compare. I was glad that Ella was staying with us for the whole week; he wouldn't try anything with her in the house.

"You don't need to tell me now, but next week when we are sitting on the beach in the middle of December you will tell me everything." I nodded my head, in agreement.

I spent the next week catering to Ella's every need. I would text Lauren pictures of her occasionally so she knew that everything was copacetic. We went shopping, and I took her to get a mini makeover.

I couldn't believe how much I loved this little girl, she made me feel young again, and having her around made it harder for me to want to leave Bo. I didn't want to give her up, and I wasn't sure I wanted to give up my dreams of living in the city with the bachelor of the year, and this perfect little girl.

Bo gave us plenty of time to spend together, since he also had to run to the office more frequently than either of us liked. Ella even came to a few of my shoots and told me she wanted to be a photographer when she grew up.

The last night before she left we were all sitting in our tent made out of blankets and sheets. We had just finished cleaning up all the popcorn from our mini food fight. I laughed so hard that I almost peed my pants, and I felt like Bo had given me the necklace that Julia Roberts got from Richard Gere in Pretty Woman.

This moment was a dream come true, and a dream that I never even wanted. It was just too perfect, and as soon as Ella drifted off to sleep I knew Bo was going to make me decide, even if he didn't know that I had a decision to make.

I heard him calling me from the bedroom. "In the kitchen, I'll be there in a minute." I finished everything up and went to be sure that Ella was sound asleep in our tent. I switched the tv off and headed for the bedroom.

I walked in and he had his reading glasses on and was reading the paper. He had no shirt and

I could see his abs from across the room. He caught me staring and patted on the bed to call me over.

"Hey pretty girl, get over here."

I climbed into the bed and threw my shirt off, leaving only the cami and my underwear on.

I let out a big yawn and felt his hand in my underwear with the exhale. Before I could stop him, I felt them gently go inside of me. I wanted to want him so bad. I wanted my life to be easy, to just stay here and never have to move all over the world or say goodbye to Jer when it came time for him to deploy.

I wanted to wake up in the city every morning, go for my run and come home to this gorgeous man and not have to worry about anything. The only problem with all of that was my heart wanted nothing to do with Bo. In fact, it ached tremendously for Jer. And although I had given Jer no promise, Bo's hands being on me felt like a sin.

"Not tonight Bo." I gently pulled his hand out and rolled over. I knew that this would be the start of the end with him. It doesn't mean that it will be the start of the beginning with Jer but I know I can't live this life with Bo, as much as my mind wanted it, my heart wouldn't budge.

I felt the silent tears on my pillow, so I turned the light off and drifted fast to sleep.

Chapter Twenty-Five

Our boarding time was way too early. At a mere 6 a.m., a time, which I had never even seen Jane awake for, was the earliest I had been up in a long time. I smiled when I saw her face light up as she ran towards me. Of course, she barely made the plane.

"Jane, so glad you could make it." I gave her an annoyed look. Even though I could hardly be upset with her at this point in time. I know how she felt with Todd, because I am sure it was very similar to the way I felt when I thought Jer wanted nothing to do with me. I looked down to turn my phone off, and felt a little bit of pain in my stomach noting there have been no calls or messages from Jer since I left that note for him.

"I seriously cannot wait to get to the beach." Jane sat down in the seat next to me and immediately covered her eyes with a fancy eye shade. "See you in a few hours bitch." I loved everything about Jane, even the parts that tend to drive me crazy, like her ability to fall asleep on a dime. And I was now left alone with my thoughts about Jer for the next six hours.

"Ahhhhh." Jane stretched out her arms, and stared out the window into the clear waters below. As much as I wanted a vacation away from everything, I had the distinct feeling that this would be more of a therapy session with Jane than anything.

I didn't want to talk about him, or Bo. I didn't want to admit that I loved him, or that maybe I didn't love him enough. I also didn't want to admit to Jane that Jer didn't come after me. I feel like that sounded so selfish, not to mention childish. But I had this vision in my head of him coming for me, all knight and shining armor like. I guess sometimes when we create the image in our heads, it makes it nearly impossible for it to happen that way and we are almost always let down.

After spending an hour getting our entire luggage, we finally made it to the condo. I took a deep breath in and tried my best to exhale all the tension that had been building up inside me.

Jane had already changed, and she came up behind me as I took in the view. "I could live here." I let out quietly. "Yeah right, you'll be begging me to take you back to the city in four days, I on the other hand could live here."

She was right. I loved the serenity, but too much of it drives me over the edge. I love to stay busy because it gives me an excuse to take my mind off of the important things.

I turned around and Jane had disappeared. As I called for her name I could hear her in the bathroom, getting sick. I knocked on the door and then quickly opened it.

"Are you ok?" She looked pitiful. "Yeah, this always happens to me when I go on vacation, I guess it's just the excitement." She wiped her mouth and brushed her teeth and glanced over at me "What? I am fine. Go to the beach. I'll meet you there."

I wasn't going to argue anymore with her. I grabbed my phone and saw two missed calls from Bo, as well as one voicemail. I pressed the play button "Hey pretty lady. I miss you already. I just dropped Ella off to Lauren. Counting down the moments until you return to me." I saved the message, and decided to turn off the phone. I knew that the one person I wanted to call me wouldn't, and I couldn't take any more disappointment this trip.

I found myself falling fast asleep in the hammock when Jane jumped in it with me. "I'm so glad we are here." She threw her arm around me. "Are you going to tell me about everything that happened with Jer or am I going to have to guess?"

I figured I might as well get it over with. I told her every detail, including our matching tattoos. "Wow B, that's some heavy shit. I mean do you really think he is the one?" I looked down at my empty ring finger. "He is the only one who could ever possibly complete me. Bo has gotten me by, and I have had so many wonderful memories with him, but the moment Jer first kissed me, it was like everything before him was a lie. I just knew."

"You mean you just know right? I mean you've told me that you want him to fight for you, but let me ask you something. Have you ever considered fighting for him?" It wasn't until those words came out of her mouth that I realized how ridiculous I had been.

"You are right. Well we have the next few days to think of an unbelievable plan, to make him forgive me for being such an ass."

"I don't think it will take much B. In fact, I don't even think you should think about it, just go with it."

"Well since you have solved all of my problems in the matter of five minutes, let's try to tackle yours." I saw her tears immediately start to fall from her eyes.

"Jane? What haven't you told me?" I was ready to kick Todd's ass, I could feel my teeth clench, and my fists in balls.

"I'm pregnant." And with those two words, I scooped up my best friend and began crying with her.

Chapter Twenty-Six

"How long have you known?" She pulled away from me. "I just took the test when we got here, but I have been in denial for about a week."

"Is that why you were really upset when I came home?" It was all making sense; Jane never acted like that about a guy. "No, I am worried, I am worried he is going to leave me. I'm going to have to raise this baby all by myself, and I am going to be miserable."

"First of all, you raising this baby all by yourself will never happen. I can promise you that. Second of all Todd will be fine with it, I am sure."

"You don't understand, he doesn't look at me the same way he did when we were out in the boondocks, I mean I feel like I was just something to pass the time while we were down there together."

"Jane, can you promise me something?" She nodded her head slowly. "Please don't overthink this until we get home. You are already at level ten, and placing that scarlet letter on your chest. Just listen to your own advice and just see where it goes." She nodded again, but I knew two things to be true, one she didn't believe me, and two my problems don't even touch hers.

The rest of our vacation was completely uneventful. We ignored the fact that Jane was carrying Todd's child. And also ignored the fact that I had no idea how to make Jer mine again, but there was no way around it, he was the one for me.

It was hard to believe that our vacation had gone by so quickly. I looked over at the again sleeping Jane on the plane. My heart warmed knowing that no matter what was in store for her, she was going to be an amazing mother. I thought of how much I loved Ella, and how no matter what we think we aren't capable of before children, it just becomes us when they enter our lives.

I was completely out of touch with Bo for the week, because I had no idea what to say to him. A part of me wanted to break it off over the phone, but that was something I would have done ten years ago, and I realized I was better than that and so was he.

I knew that I wasn't ruining a dream for either of us. Although Bo and I could probably go on forever the way we were, it would merely be for the comfort. I didn't want a mediocre love, and unfortunately if Bo and I stayed together, that was all it would ever be.

We finally landed and Todd would be picking us up from the airport. Jane's anxiety peaked a new level. We decided on the last day of vacation that she was going to wait until after her first doctor's appointment to tell Todd. She still didn't believe the ten other tests that we had purchased on vacation. I assured her that it was normal to be in denial, and that if she needed to wait to tell him that was fine. I think more or less she wanted to see how he was with her without knowing about the pregnancy first.

As we got off the plane, my eyes searched for Todd but instead they rested on Bo. I saw him mouth to me "hey pretty lady." He looked amazing. My mind forgot of the spell he could put on me with his looks alone. He came up to me and wrapped his arms around and lifted me off the ground.

"I've missed you." I don't know why those were the first words to leave my mouth, but it just felt natural. I closed my eyes and wished it was Jer, but then it hit me. Maybe that's all I'll ever be doing is wishing. It's an unrealistic scenario, he and I. After just talking myself into fighting for him, the other part of me, the part embraced by Bo talked myself right out of it.

The choice of Jer was illogical, and hasty. Who knew if it wasn't just lust, or the desire to have him because I couldn't stand the thought of him being with anyone else? I was being selfish, and if he hadn't come after me, maybe he realized that long before I did.

"Baby, I've got us dinner reservations, you must be starving?" I nodded in agreement, and I turned to find Jane.

I saw Todd with his arms placed around her. Gently pressing his lips to her forehead, I saw her start to tear up. She looked over at me and I mouthed, *get it together.* She smiled and broke away to just stare at him. I wasn't sure if it was my imagination, because I wasn't even sure it was possible for either of them, but I think they were falling in love.

I know it would take a lot to convince Jane of this little fact, which I knew to be true by the way, that Todd looked at her, but eventually she would figure it out for herself.

I walked out front and saw the limo, and my heart started beating a little faster. I looked down at myself, and then looked up at Bo. "I'm going to need a shower, and definitely some decent clothes." He smiled "Of course baby, I have everything ready for you at our place."

The way he said *our place* made it sound like he had just won a prize. We got in the limo, and he started slowly kissing me immediately, as much as I wanted to fight it, I didn't. It had been exactly 14 days 4 hours and 32 minutes since I had seen or heard from Jer. In that moment I allowed myself to let go of that fantasy I had been holding onto.

As we pulled up to the apartment I ran inside to get a quick shower and ready as fast as possible. Bo told me he had some business calls to make so he would just wait in the car, and although he mentioned not to rush, I couldn't help but feel the pressure to be as fast as possible.

I looked over at the clock when I was finished, and did a little clap for myself when I realized I had set a new record for getting ready. Bo had laid out a brand-new dress, along with shoes, and accessories for me to wear and they were all gorgeous, meaning that his assistant had put in some extra time over the weekend.

This wasn't the first time Bo had done this for me, and he wasn't aware that I figured out one of his assistants put in "extra hours" to accomplish this. Last year at his Christmas party she let it slip, and I couldn't be more pleased with her sense in style. I have continued to keep my lips sealed, and every time I get another surprise like this I squeal in delight, and quietly of course.

Finally, after I pulled the silk black dress over my curves, I glanced in the mirror at the back of the dress, which dipped down in an extremely low V. I smiled and threw on some flip flops, and threw the six-inch heels in my purse, I didn't want to overdo myself before I even got to dinner.

As I got in the limo Bo looked over at me, and I thought I saw his mouth drop just a little. "I have to call you back." He slammed the phone shut. This was not normal Bo behavior but I liked it.

Without saying a word, he grabbed my hand and pulled me on top of him. He placed his strong hand on my jaw and pulled me in for a kiss. There was something different in Bo's kiss, maybe longing? I mean it had only been a week apart and we have surely done it before, but it was just different.

"I'm sorry." He looked at my eyes when he said it, and I was sure that the look on my face was something along the lines of confused.

"Bells, I have never realized how much I have loved you until I thought you weren't mine anymore." He took a deep breath in and I knew that there was more coming, but I was confused at how he knew that my heart wasn't all the way his. I hadn't told him anything about my trip back home with Jer, maybe he was assuming with my actions?

"I've never realized the way you light up in response to me putting my arms around you. The way I feel when I have you in my presence. I've always been so afraid to fall in love with you, and afraid to let you all the way in. I knew for a long time that I loved you, but I wasn't sure in which way. That is until I saw you with my daughter." I smiled, thinking of Ella.

"And then I realized, I am in love with you. Madly, passionately, want to have babies with you in love with you." I felt my stomach squeeze, and I wasn't sure the emotion it was producing.

"I've waited far too long, and I am sorry for that. But I've come to realize, I cannot live without you."

He slid me off of him and in the limo got down on one knee.

"Would you make me the luckiest man, and become my wife, the mother of my children, and my forever?"

I looked at him and then down at the ring, which was an amazing 3-karat princess cut. I didn't know what to do; I felt the adrenaline in my body start to build up. My fight or flight kicked in and I realized I couldn't go anywhere, I felt trapped. And then I said, "Yes." And it was like I was freed.

I didn't have time to process what I was thinking, or feeling. I didn't have time to think about Jer, and how this would crush him, or maybe this would also set him free.

I wasn't concerned if it were mediocre because maybe everything for Jer was just magnified in the moment, maybe it would dissolve over time. I couldn't stop living my life for him, especially when he didn't come for me.

So right now, I was deciding to let myself be happy with Bo. Let myself have the happily ever after, that I often didn't think I even deserved.

Chapter Twenty-Seven
Six Months Later

"This is no fun!" Jane was whining in the waiting area, as I tried on the fourth dress of the morning. None of them seemed to be perfect, and I just wanted perfect.

I peeked out behind the drapes, and saw her with her feet on the couch, playing on her phone like she was five years old. I glanced at her little growing bump, and saw her place her hand over top of it.

"Alright I am coming out, but this is the last one of the days, and I assure you it is not the one!" I came out and did a spin, Jane stuck her tongue out in agreement. We both started laughing, and I walked over to the couch and sat beside her with the oversized dress.

"What am I doing Jane?" I looked defeated, I could tell by her reaction. "Don't start with me B! I am huge, and miserable right now, my feet are starting to swell and I am constantly tired. You on the other hand are engaged to the hottest bachelor, who will do whatever it takes to make you happy. I DO NOT WANT TO HEAR IT!"

Jane had been helping me plan the wedding since the night I had accepted Bo's proposal. I promised that we would have plenty of time since we planned on waiting for the arrival of my God daughter. That was the first question out of Jane's mouth when she found out about the engagement, which was the day after it happened. I knew she probably wouldn't even come to the wedding if she was pregnant, which gave me the perfect excuse to draw out our engagement.

Since that night, everything with Bo remained somewhat magical. It was almost as if I was engaged to a figment of my imagination. He catered to my beck and call, and gave me compliments every day when he came home from work.

He made dinner most nights, rubbed my feet, and then we had sex, every single night, religiously. Of course, the night of our proposal I came home and told Bo everything that happened between Jer and I. I told him I didn't want to base our engagement on any false pretenses. I was actually surprised that he didn't get mad. I almost expected him to take the ring off my finger and call it off.

Instead he looked sad, but then shot a smile at me and pulled me in for a hug. I cried for what seemed like forever, and for many reasons. Part of me was happy that Bo wanted to be with me for the rest of his life, and the other part of me, which always seemed to be the bigger part, was sad that Jer didn't. The biggest part of me was sad that I still hadn't even heard from him, and I felt like I had betrayed him.

Jane has talked me out of this guilt on the regular, but it always resurfaces. Now it has been over a half of a year, and I have no idea what Jer is doing, or where he is for that matter. Not a letter, postcard, text. Nothing.

On the surface I know I appear to be happy, to be grateful, and completely in love with Bo, but below is still that longing pain for Jer. I always thought he would be my knight in shining armor, my Richard Gere that rode in the white limo to save the day, but these were simply unrealistic expectations···a figment of my imagination.

I also found myself replaying that night with Jer and I in bed, maybe I thought it was more magical than it actually was. Maybe I created this picture of how I thought it should be and just made it happen. But at the end of the day, I cannot convince myself that it was a dream, or illusion. It was real, and he had my whole heart for my whole life, and what he decided to do with it, was hand it over to Bo.

I snapped back to reality. "I know, no complaining, you win you are growing my favorite person in the entire world." I put my hand on the belly, and felt a little jealous.

"Well what are we doing tonight for dinner?" She was hungry, and therefore getting grumpy.

"Whatever you like princess!" I directed that at her belly as well. "What I would like, is for Todd to grow the fuck up and put a ring on my finger." And here we go. Jane and Todd have been camped out in my old apartment, he has been modeling on the regular for George and never home. He also shows no signs of putting a ring on her finger anytime in the near future. But I give him props for being able to listen to her complains about not getting a ring.

I know that Jane feels huge, and unlovable and so not sexy, but she is gorgeous and glowing. No pregnant woman wants to really hear that they are glowing, so I decided to keep that part to myself.

I understand the pressure she feels because Todd has not committed to her, to continue to be beautiful and try to not be a complete bitch, I also know that some days this is a true struggle for her.

I took off the dress and threw on my oversized t-shirt and ripped jean shorts, threw my hair back up in a bun and had to wake sleeping beauty off of the couch.

"Let's do dinner at our place tonight, I'll have Bo order something in though."
"I would love that. Just text Todd and tell him to meet us there." I grabbed her phone and whispered lazy ass under my breath, sometimes I swear she thinks I am her personal assistant.

I picked up her phone and followed her out of the store. When I unlocked the phone her call log appeared. I felt my lunch coming up when I saw the number that had appeared from two days ago.

"Jane." I couldn't even get anything else out, and I literally felt my legs giving out on me. I leaned against the building, numb to all of the sounds of the city. She looked at me as I dropped her phone, and I saw in her eyes that she knew.

"B, it's not what you think. Calm down." How could she? I would recognize the number anywhere because I had dialed it over a million times in my life. It was Jer's. I pulled the phone to my view again and she tried to snatch it out of my hands.

"Get the fuck away from me." I said it lowly, and I grabbed the phone up. I saw that the call lasted 8 minutes and 14 seconds.

"Why? Why would you call him?" she tried to step towards me again and I put my hand up.

"B, I was just. Ugh you won't understand anyway!" She grabbed her phone out of my hands and stormed off. I lowered myself to the ground and sat on the busy seat of New York feeling empty and numb.

Chapter Twenty-Eight

It has been one week since I have seen or heard from Jane. This was the longest we had gone without speaking to one another. My daily routine was all that kept me going; I literally went through the motions every day without deviating.

Bo was unaware of why we got into the argument, and I am pretty sure he knew that it was not up for discussion right now.

The hardest part about the whole situation is that Jane didn't even tell me what they were talking about, which left my mind wandering all day long. I wondered if he knew that I was getting married, if he had met someone.

This was the conclusion that I came up with at the end of every day because I knew that she wouldn't want to tell me, because she knew it would break my heart.

How could I be such a hypocrite? I needed to get some air so instead of going to work I decided to call out.

Halfway through my run, I let my emotions take over, and they led me to Jane's door. I was sweaty, and gross. As I went to knock on her door I turned around. For some reason I couldn't go through with it. I hated confrontation and conflict my entire life. Jane knew this, and was probably planning on using it to her advantage. I was sure that she was waiting on me to come over and do exactly this.

I wasn't this time. Whatever was said between she and Jer she had days to mention it to me, and that hurt more than anything.

As I was jogging down the stairs and staring at my feet I ran straight into someone.

Without looking up I said sorry, and moved to the side.

"It's ok." I felt my body tense up, and it took all the willpower I had to pull my eyes away from my feet.

He was wearing a baseball hat, loose fitted t-shirt that hugged his arms, and a pair of dark denim jeans. He was somehow more beautiful that I had imagined possible. My body was frozen, as was my mind.

He pulled me into his chest, and as a reflex my arms went around his body. I pulled away to look at him, surely, I was just dehydrated and this was a hallucination.

"How are you here?" I said them quietly and more to myself than to him. I couldn't remember all the anger I had stored up for this moment, the disappointment I felt because he didn't come after me.

"Because I came to get you." He whispered into my ear. I instantly realized that the magic that I had convinced myself into thinking was my imagination was far from it. Just his whisper set my body on fire.

"Let's go get some fresh air." I was trying to put everything together. I looked up at Jane's door and then looked back at him. I was trying to solve the puzzle without having all of the pieces.

He held my hand and practically pulled me out of the building. We held hands and walked five blocks to a small outdoor café. I don't think until that moment that I had ever truly experienced shock. I had so many things to say but I would open my mouth and none of them would fall out.

We sat down, and I immediately became aware of the fact that I smelled disgusting. I was sure he saw me make the face and he replied to it "You smell fine! And you look amazing. Stop." It was more playful than anything, and so familiar. Like no time had passed at all.

"How?" That was all I could manage to get out.

"Well, that's kind of a loaded question huh?" He laughed nervously. "I'm assuming you mean how did I get here? As in New York?" He was also rambling which I knew meant he was nervous. I had always pictured everything about him feeling foreign when I saw him again, but it was all the same. He somehow had gotten more attractive, but he was the same.

"I'm assuming Bo didn't fill you in on my visit here when you were in The Keys?" He picked up my hand.

"What are you talking about?" I was getting more of those pieces. "Iz, I came for you. I fought for you. After getting your letter that morning, I knew you needed space. I knew that you needed to just breathe. I gave it a week, and then I came here. I came for you." He looked down at my hand and saw the engagement ring, and let go.

"When I got to your place, Bo welcomed me in, which I should have taken as the first clue. He obviously didn't know anything about what happened, but he did when I left. He told me·····..He told me." I could hear the hurt in his voice.

"He told me you came back and accepted his proposal. Iz, I left that day with my heart shattered across your floor."

"We weren't engaged, not then anyway." I was being very direct, because I didn't know what else to do.

"I know that now, thanks to Jane. I've been in my own hell for 7 months."

"I didn't think you came after me."

"It shouldn't have even been a thought!" He was pissed now.

"I fucking loved you more than I ever loved anyone in my life and you didn't even wait a fucking month to get engaged to that bag of douche." Jer was emotional; I could feel it in his voice.

"Jer. I have so much to say to you, and I don't even know where to start." I rubbed my face with my hands, and I could see him flinch at the sight of my ring. I flipped the diamond around so only the thin band was showing.

"What you felt for me? What you said that night, what happened between us was it real?" I felt angry with myself for making him question that.

"Jer, it was as real as it gets. I almost thought that I had imagined everything, then today just by touching me it all came back."

"I feel it too." He reached for my hands again. I felt bad for being so angry with Jane.

"Jane called me because she said I couldn't let you go through with it. She couldn't let you marry him. She told me about the keys, and how you were devastated that I didn't call you or come after you. The reason I didn't call was because I thought you were already engaged to him. I thought you had already given up on me. And you didn't call me either, I should add!"

His emotions were teetering back and forth between happiness, sadness, and anger. I felt the same way.

"I guess we are both just stubborn as hell." Thank god for Jane. My first stop after this was to her; the second was to kill Bo for pushing Jer away.

Now that I am sitting across from him, I knew I had many choices to make. The first was to take off my ring, so I did so right in front of Jer. As far as I was concerned, I did not belong to Bo and I was pretty sure I never did.

"So where does this leave us?" I asked and stared right into those amazing blue eyes.

"I hope it leaves you with me. I know that you have a lot to deal with right now, I am staying at The Plaza, meet me there when you're ready." He slid the key over. "I'm not going anywhere until you tell me to."

I nodded and started to get up. He grabbed my hand and pulled me into him. I felt his muscular body under his shirt and I wanted to rip it right off of him. He pulled me in and his lips grazed mine. At first he was gentle, almost asking permission. I pushed all of my weight into him and let my tongue slipped into his mouth. He matched all of my moves, making it nearly impossible to pull apart from him.

"I love you." He whispered into my ear, I could melt at the way his hand was cupping my jaw. I said it right back as he stared into my eyes. He is my home, and I almost forgot how homesick I was.

Chapter Twenty-Nine

I changed my mind; my first stop was to Bo. Without even showering I ran my ass right to his office. I didn't care if I stank when I was telling him off. I had only been in his office one other time, and it was because he asked me to meet him there. I walked in to the receptionist, and she smiled warmly at me. She knew who I was.

"Oh I don't think Mr. Bronson is expecting you, but he just got done a meeting, you have a few minutes until his next, go right in!"

"Thanks, it will only take a few minutes." I walked right past her.

I opened the door and saw him relaxing in his chair with his legs up on the desk. It made me feel even more ready to tell him off.

"Baby, what a nice surprise. You know I always wanted to fuck you on my desk!" Ugh. I couldn't even stand the thought of him at the moment.

"Shut your fucking mouth Robert." I never, ever called him by his real name and I could see how uncomfortable it made him. "I like it when you talk dirty baby, but you know I hate my real name."

"You're right I do know that, which is exactly why I used it. How about you tell me why I'm here right now!"

"Ummmm I'm not sure." He was trying to play it cool, and I was not in the mood for it. "I want my shit packed and ready for me to pick up on Friday." I slid the ring on his desk and he still looked confused. I bent over and stared him in the eyes "Jer."

All the color washed out of his face. He didn't say anything and I didn't expect him to. I knew that he could tell how devastated I was the week that I came home, and I couldn't believe how selfish he was to send Jer away like that.

I was never one to storm out of a room, but I felt that I was rather successful at this one. Just when I had reached the elevator I heard his voice from behind me. "I'm not going to make a scene in my office, but I did this for you!"

I turned around, knowing that I had never been so angry in my life. "How dare you say that to me? You knew that I loved him, and if you didn't know that you knew that he was my best friend, and you stripped me of that! I will never forgive you for that. EVER!"

"Well maybe you should ask Jer what really happened between he and Melissa, then you'll be begging me to accept your forgiveness."

The elevator opened at that moment, thank God and I left.

I was literally a mess. Still no shower, I sent my assistant to get some clothes from Bo's apartment. Sitting on Jane's couch with ice cream sounded like the best place for me to be right now. I wasn't ready to see Jer yet, mostly because I wasn't showered but partially because of what Bo said.

After a million apologies from me, Jane finally told me to shut up. "Well let's get to the bottom of this Melissa story. What would Bo know that you wouldn't?"

"I don't know that's the problem. I mean I could just call Jer and I am sure he would tell me, but am I ready for whatever it is? Bo made it seem horrendous."

"Well Bo is also an asshole." Valid point Jane.

So tonight it's just me Jane, her little nugget and Ben and Jerry for me. Two of my favorite men, they never complain or ask questions, and I just pour out my soul to them.

After showering and falling asleep watching reruns of I love Lucy, I was woken up by fumbling at the door. At first it scared the shit out of me, but once I rolled over to see Jane sleeping alone in her bed I knew who it was.

I quietly opened the door and saw Todd, with his arm wrapped around the broad shoulders of Bo. It was one of those moments where I wasn't sure if I was dreaming, so I took a step back and tried to wipe the sleep from my eyes.

I heard Bo whispering to Todd, who was clearly smashed. "Is this where I drop off lost and found items?" Bo chuckled.

"Shut up or you will wake up Jane." I looked at Todd, and instantly felt hurt for Jane. She didn't deserve this, and I knew this wasn't a rare occurrence. Todd looked too seasoned, and it became evident that this was a nightly routine.

I looked at Todd in the eye, "Get your ass in the shower. NOW." I think it was the first time I spoke to him like this, and he looked a little scared.

He stood straight up and saluted me as he walked into the bathroom. Bo tried to come in right behind him. I shoved my arm in front of him. "Absolutely not."

"Come on baby, you know you'll be back in my arms in a matter of days why waste time?"

"And why exactly would I be back in your arms Bo?" I could tell by his speech he was also feeling a little more than buzzed.

"Because you are going to find out that Jer got Melissa pregnant!" he finished with a hiccup. I wasn't sure if this was a story or factual, and how Bo would even know this information. I knew that I had based too many of my decisions on what Bo had shared, or decided not to share with me so I tried not to get my emotions involved at all.

"Bo you are drunk, I will call you a cab." I started to close the door. "Ask him Bells, she's about due around the time of your Goddaughter. How ironic?"

"That's it Bo. Get the fuck out now, or I will call the police."

With that empty threat, Bo turned and left. I went to check on Todd who seemed to be sobering up.

I cracked the door open, feeling slightly overwhelmed. "Todd⋯."

"Yeahhhhh?"

"Please don't break her heart."

"Roger that."

I didn't want to be in the apartment when Todd came out, in case I decided to become verbal with him. I was irritated that he thought he could just come and go as he pleased without taking care of the mother of his child.

I started to ponder the chances of Jer being a father to Melissa's baby. Would I be able to stay with him? Just when I accepted the fact that I would move anywhere in the world for him, I was possibly thrown another obstacle.

I think as women, we sometimes push ourselves to the limit if we want something so bad. The pair of jeans that are just one size too small, or the pair of shoes that may max out our credit cards. We know that there are things we shouldn't have, because they will make our lives more difficult, but we choose them anyway.

This is the only explanation that I see for Jane and Todd's relationship. She knows he probably isn't good for her; in fact realistically he is probably the worst for her right now. But she chooses him, because she wants it badly.

As I found myself walking on the streets of New York, at 4 am with my Plaza key in hand, I wondered what I was going to choose. How much would be too much?

Chapter Thirty

I pushed the door open slowly. I was amazed at how beautiful the room was. I saw him sound asleep in the bed, and I almost questioned if I wanted to wake him.

I took everything off except for my bra and panties, I knew that I hadn't decided if I would stay, but I knew I wasn't leaving without being with him, even if it would be our last time.

I climbed in the bed and faced him. He looked so peaceful; I almost wanted to just sleep right beside him. I wanted to wake up in his arms, and pretend that we never left each other's side.

He slowly opened his eyes. "Iz?" It wasn't so much a question as it was a statement.

I nodded slowly and he pulled me into him. Without asking him any questions or ruining the moment, I fell into a deep kiss.

I felt his hands feverishly trying to find the clasp on my bra, I felt the smile in his kiss when he was successful. He placed his hands all over me, without moving his lips away.

Finally breaking apart he leaned into my ear and whispered *I Love You.* I wanted him so badly I couldn't wait. I pulled the covers over my head, and went down on him.

I could hear his gentle moans encouraging me to go faster. I followed his cues, and enjoyed feeling him pulsate in my mouth. "Baby, you have to stop or I'm going to⋯."

I felt him pull me up and I stared into his eyes, this man was my forever. "Is it ok? I don't have any condoms." I nodded my head and felt him ease inside of me. It sent sparks through my body, and I instantly felt my body shaking from the sensation.

"What are you doing to me?" I asked in his ear, barely able to speak at all. He flipped me over in one fluid motion, and whispered back. "I'm making you mine." I laid on my back staring up at him, taking in everything about him. His ice blue eyes, I rubbed my hands along his chest and then across his abs. I finally reached both hands behind and grabbed his ass.

"I'm going to cum baby⋯where?"

I felt my climax coming, and couldn't speak so I just nodded.

"Are you sure?"

"Yesssss!" I felt myself exploding on him. I grabbed a pillow to muffle the sounds of my screams, and I felt his whole body tighten, and then become limp on top of me.

"You are amazing Iz." I kissed him on the forehead still unable to even speak.

I had no idea it was even possible to feel this way. I was in such a euphoric state, and felt like no matter what situation we found ourselves in; I needed to be with him.

"If I ask you something, will you promise not to run?" As he said the words I knew he could feel my body tighten under his hands. He was going to tell me that Melissa was pregnant.

"I promise you." I had myself convinced that I could love him through it.

He looked so nervous, so I placed my hands on either side of his face and pulled him into another kiss. Finally, he pulled away, "I'll be right back. Close your eyes"

I did as he said, and closed my eyes. I couldn't believe it was 4 am and I was naked, in a hotel room with Jer. My whole world changed in a matter of 24 hours.

"Don't peek."

"Ok. I won't."

I felt his lips caress my hip bones, and travel up my stomach. In between kisses he would say a word or two.

"Iz, you are my everything." Another kiss, this one just below my breast and I felt myself getting excited all over again.

"If there is one thing I know for sure⋯" and his mouth was on my breasts, causing a quick exhale, and almost a squeal.

"It's that I need you to be mine." I felt his lips on my neck.

"Forever." On my lips.

"You can open your eyes." As I opened my eyes I looked at Jer who was lying next to me, with a diamond ring in his hand.

"I know that a lot has happened in the past 6 months, but you still know me better than anyone. I can't stand one more minute of you not being mine. Will you marry me?"

"Yes!" My heart was in total control of my mind.

"But I have a question for you. How long have you had that ring?"

"I brought it with me when I came to get you, I was going to ask you six months ago, but someone beat me to the punch."

He grabbed my hand and placed the ring on my finger. When I looked down at it, for the first time really, I felt the tears stream down my face.

"Are you sure you want to give me this ring?" I knew that his mother had this ring since she was a teenager herself, a family heirloom that had been handed down for generations.

"When I asked my mom for the ring, she told me she always knew it belonged to you."

I jumped on top of him, and put everything Bo had ever said out of my mind. At this moment I was exactly where I was supposed to be, it just took me a little longer to get there.

Chapter Thirty-One

When morning came, I woke up wrapped up in sheets and Jer's arms. We needed a day alone to figure everything out, and waking up I knew I couldn't wait another minute to ask him about Melissa.

"Good morning babe. I've already called for room service."
"Ah you know me so well! Pancake Sunday?"
"Of course, sorry I can't make them myself today."
"I guess I will have to suck it up and deal with whatever the 5 star restaurant whips up." I crossed my arms and he began laughing. I patted my hand on the bed next to me inviting him over.

"I need to ask you something." He didn't look like he was expecting this to come out of my mouth.

"Melissa is pregnant." I said it as if it were gospel. He nodded his head.
"And it's yours isn't it?" He turned to face me.
"Are you seriously asking me if I got Melissa pregnant and didn't tell you already?"

"Well didn't you? I mean who else would be the father."
"First and foremost, thank you for accepting my proposal based on the fact that you thought I had knocked up some girl already. You must really love me." I nodded and rolled into him. If it wasn't evident that he owned me by now, I don't know that it ever would be.

"Jer after everything we've been through, I don't think anything could keep me away from you." He placed a quick kiss on my forehead and I felt him melt into me.

"Well babe, I feel the same way about you. But unfortunately, I cannot tell you who the father is."

"You don't know?" I pulled away staring into his eyes.
"Oh, I know, I just know you won't be able to keep your mouth shut and right now is not the time."
" I can to keep my mouth shut!"

"Will you please just trust me, you need to just give it some time."

"Jer, you are testing me!" I tried to sound irritated, but my euphoria was overcasting any other emotion within me.

"I know babe. Let's just have this day for us, to celebrate where we finally are, it took us six months of hell to get here."

"Ok, but tomorrow you are telling me."
"Fine."

I spent half of my morning just lying next to Jer. I know we had a lot to iron out over the next few months, like if I was going to move to Virginia with him right away, or stay here for a while and commute. I've already thought about the drive, and it wouldn't be horrible. I assumed he would be in constant training anyway.

I can't believe that he actually joined the military. I thought for sure he would just tuck the dream to the back, file it away. I had no idea what his job entailed, and I had a feeling it was one of those jobs I would never know much about. I knew everything there was to know about him, and the first and foremost is that Jer is secretly Clark Kent, and I am sure that he will be doing nothing mediocre with his life.

"What's on your mind Iz?" He interrupted my thoughts, and startled me a bit.

"Nothing, just picturing our lives together. Where do you see us over the next year?"

"I see you, in the kitchen of the home I bought for us in a quiet town. I see me coming home every single night, and never ever taking for granted that you are there waiting for me."

This boy that I grew up with, is such a wonderful man now. I'm almost proud of who he has become, because whether we give each other credit or not, I think that we helped each other get here; to this very moment, where we are completely in love, and appreciate each other.

I always felt that appreciation is the biggest part of a relationship, and that is something I know I will always feel for Jer.

"What is your work schedule going to be like? Will I ever get to see you?"

"Every second I get, I'll be home with you."

"Well since I know you so well, I'll take that as I won't be seeing much of you."

"Not for the next year and a half or so. I'll be doing a lot of training. But you'll always be here." He put his hand on his heart. I smacked his hand "Quit being corny!" He smirked at me, and I knew that he was just trying to lighten the mood.

"I am sorry that I am asking you to do this." He whispered.

"Do you love what you do?"

"Yes."

"Do you love me?"

"Yes."

"Then don't ever be sorry. You can have everything you want, and you should never apologize for it!"

The rest of the morning we finished making plans for our lives. Including the wedding that we would be having in our hometown in four months. Jer also agreed that it was fair for us to commute while he is in training. So that meant I would be kicking Jane out of my apartment, and moving back in.

I was glad that he wasn't asking me to leave everything that I had loved, at least right away. I know that photography is something that I could take anywhere, but I just wasn't sure I wanted to leave just yet.

We spent the rest of the day walking through the city together. And although sites that had the capability of consuming the hearts of so many tourists surrounded us, Jer and I stared at each other. I saw him in the same way as a virgin New Yorker. With awe, the hope for something amazing to happen, the motivation to work hard to get there, but most of all the passion that ties it all together.

As dinnertime was quickly approaching, I picked up my phone to call Jane and check in on her.

"Jane, I said yes!!!!"

"Oh. My. Gosh! I knew it, you two are meant to be together. I can't even stand it. And by the way how is it that you get two men to propose to you and I can't even get one?"

"It will happen Jane, just give him time."

"Thanks for taking care of him last night by the way, ugh. It's been exhausting to say the least."

"No problem lady, plus I owed you anyway. Hey why don't you guys meet us for dinner in an hour?"

"I would love to! Text me where and see you then."

I felt Jer behind me before I heard him.

"Who was that?"

"Jane and Todd are meeting us for dinner." I felt his arms pull away from me.

I turned to look at him and I could tell he was uncomfortable.

"What's wrong babe?"

"I think it's time we had that talk."

Chapter Thirty-Two

Jer pulled me through the city, like he had lived here his whole life. We were back in the hotel room. I had no idea why this matter was so urgent, and why he felt the need to bring me 27 blocks back to our hotel to tell me.

He was pacing across the floor, and running his fingers through his hair.
He always seemed composed, even in the most stressful situations so now I was feeding off of his anxiety. I just noticed the five o'clock shadow on his face, which made him all the more appealing to me. I had to pull my mind away from all of the things I wanted to do to him, to figure out why he brought me here.

"Jer start talking right now. You are freaking me the fuck out!"
"I don't know how to tell you this. Because I know you are going to be pissed that I have known, and haven't done something about it, but I just didn't know what to do.
I mean there's nothing I could do and I didn't want her heart to be ripped out."

"What the hell are you talking about just spit it out already!" I raised my voice, which was now shaking.

"Todd is the one who got Melissa pregnant." He took a deep breath like the weight had been taken off of his shoulders, and I immediately felt it transfer to mine.

"What do you mean?" I said the words through my teeth, I wasn't angry with Jer, but I was angry at the situation. Beyond angry, because he was right this would rip her heart out.

"Ok so when you all came down there, and you know things between Melissa and I kind of dissolved, well she hooked up with Todd."
"How do you know it's not yours?" At this point, strangely enough I almost wished that it were Jer's because if it really were Todd's this would crush

Jane. And I didn't know if I had the heart to tell her now, while she was carrying the baby.

"Trust me I am positive it's not mine."

"Jer, I need more information than that, I mean it was what a few weeks difference if that. It could be yours."

"Iz, I never slept with her."

"But I thought···you said she was the one." I know that my face reflected the confusion I was feeling. "I was acting like a teenage boy, we both know she wasn't the one. You have always been the one. And I couldn't sleep with her, not once I realized that you were all I wanted."

I was relieved that he hadn't slept with her, and I was pissed that she slept with Todd. I wanted to get in the car and drive straight home and find her. I knew she rubbed me the wrong way, I just didn't expect it to be this way.

"You can't." I almost wondered if what I had just thought I was saying out loud, but I realized that Jer was exceptionally good at reading my mind.

I started to cry. He came over and put his hand on my shoulder and pulled me in.

"I know babe, I feel the same way." It was probably true that he felt the same way, but Jer was almost like a vampire in the way he could turn his emotions off.

"Now what do we do?"

"Well I confronted Todd when I first got into town. He knows it's his, but now he knows that I know it's his."

"That explains the drinking, and probably why Bo told me you got Melissa pregnant."

"In all fairness I don't blame Bo for believing that it was mine, I am sure half of the people at home think it's mine."

"Who is she saying the father is?"

"She is saying that it is someone that she met on a whim, and he isn't involved."

"Well duh everyone thinks it's you!" I tugged at my hair in frustration. The only crisis manager I knew was Jane, and surely, she couldn't fix her own crisis.

He nodded and my heart broke for him. I was angrier than ever with Melissa. I looked at my watch and saw that it was time to meet Jane and Todd for dinner.

"Give me a few minutes to get myself together, I'm not going to be able to ignore him, then she will definitely suspect something."

After taking a few deep breaths, and freshly applying makeup I felt a little better. I had no idea how to act normal around Todd now, because I knew too much.

Part of me wished Jer didn't tell me. Ignorance is bliss, but at least I had the upper hand in knowing the truth.

I stepped out of the bathroom and Jer pulled me right into him.

"I've never felt so right, so at home as I do right now." He ran his finger down my side and I felt his hand at the hem of my dress.

Slowly he started inching it up and I felt my panties slowly falling to my ankles. If there were one thing to get my mind off of the whole situation, this would be it.

I pressed my back into the wall as Jer dropped to his knees. I felt his lips on my inner thigh and I wanted to scream. His tongue fluttered just beside me, and then finally I felt him on me.

I let out a sharp exhale and stared down at him. I felt his finger rub my clit as his tongue fluttered on me simultaneously.

I pulled his hair softly, my legs now shaking. He pulled away and smiled up at me, fully aware of what he was doing to me. I was unraveling right in front of him.

"Cancel." He said in between my legs, and handed me the phone.

"I···I··· can't, she needs me."

"You need this more." No one has ever been so right about anything.

"You have to stop while I call her. I won't be able to······" He felt amazing.

"You won't be able to finish your sentence?"

I nodded and he pulled away, keeping his hands on my hips I felt his head lean against my stomach.

She answered on the first ring. "Jane, I'm so sorry I'm not going to be able to make it."

"Are you fucking kidding me?" I would normally blame her pregnancy hormones, but I knew this was entirely my fault.

"I'm sorry, I'm just not feeling well."
"I'm calling your bluff, I know you are just fucking him. Well at least one of us is getting some. You owe me big time bitch, call me tomorrow!"

"I will Jane, we need to talk about something anyway."

She hung up and I could feel her irritation, but I could also feel Jer back on me and nothing in the world mattered anymore.

<u>Chapter Thirty-Three</u>

After another amazing night with him, I couldn't help but wonder if I would ever get sick of him. I softly stroked his arm and kissed his bareback. I could feel him start to stir.

"Good morning sweetheart." He gave me that crooked smile that I knew I couldn't live without.

"Hey. So today is going to be a busy one for me. I have to see Jane, I have to work and I have to go get some clothes from Bo to last me until the weekend."

His eyes were closing again; I knew he wouldn't be fully awake until he had his morning coffee. So I told him to go back to sleep and I would call him later. I doubt if he heard me, so I left a note as well.

I quietly left the room, and entered the chaos of the city. I felt euphoric, like I could conquer the world, which was a great feeling since today that is precisely what I had to do.

I still had no clue how to deal with Jane, so I decided to head to Bo's first.

As I stood out front I wondered if he had already left for work, rather than knocking I used my key and quietly slipped in the door.

I heard the flipping of papers and I peeked into the kitchen and saw Bo, shirtless with his immaculate abs, the stubble that was barely noticeable across his face, the dark wavy hair with his hand running effortlessly through it.

"You should have knocked."

"I am sorry Bo, I didn't expect you to be here. I just need to grab a few things."

"We have a problem."

"We don't have anything anymore Bo, you may have a problem but I am certainly not a part of it."

"Ella is coming to visit this weekend, she doesn't know about us being apart, and I honestly think she would be more excited to see you than me. I've got tickets to a show, and I promise to be a complete gentleman."

This was something that I didn't have an answer for. Although it should be an obvious no, I just couldn't bring myself to mouth the words. I could feel her disappointment, and picture the look on her face. I couldn't do that to her.

"Bo, I can't give you an answer right now. I need to talk to Jer."

He looked down at the paper, and mumbled something under his breath.

" Bo, he is not the father of that baby, you and I both know it. He has done nothing to you, in fact he should hate you but he doesn't."

"Ah, then he is the better man because I sure do hate him." I almost felt sorry for Bo, almost.

"Well I'm going to get my things, I'll text you later about this weekend. Don't get your hopes up, you better have a backup plan."

"I always do. By the way, you were always my first choice. Jer may not be the father of that baby, but he certainly didn't choose you over her. She left him for Todd."

That thought had never crossed my mind, and I let it bother me. The moment he said it I questioned its validity.

"Bo, I was always his first choice he just didn't know that he was mine too."

I lied right to his face. Why does he have the ability to make me question all of my beliefs? He knew he did it too, even though I spat the words right back at him, he knew he hit a nerve. We had spent too much time together for him to not know it.

"I'll be seeing you Bells."

I grabbed my bag of necessities and hailed a cab to my old apartment. I decided on the way that unless I had no reasonable doubts whatsoever could I tell Jane about Todd being the father. Not only could it possibly ruin her relationship with him, it could also stress the baby. I was being such a hypocrite considering how devastated I was when I found out that she had withheld information from me, but I had to choose the lesser of the evils, and today that was not telling her.

I finally made it to her door, and let myself in. The apartment was empty except the light from the bathroom, which I assumed, was occupied.

"Biotch, I am here getting ready. I need to head to the studio if you want to tag along."

"I'm good, I've got some errands to run today but feel free to call me bitch anytime you like." His joking manner made me even more disgusted with him.

"Todd clearly that invite was not made for you, in fact I don't even want you within ten feet of me."

"Shut up!" He still thought I was kidding around with him.

"When is the due date again?" He replied with Jane's due date.

I eyed him up and down. "And the other baby, when is that one due."

He looked as if he had swallowed his own tongue. I could see the fear in his face. I wasn't sure if he was more upset that he got caught, or that he was going to hurt Jane. I was really pulling for the latter of the two.

"I'm going to tell her. Melissa means nothing to me! And I swear it's not even my baby."

"Did you sleep with her?" He nodded. "Did you use a condom?" He was silent and still. "It could be Jer's baby!!!" He almost screamed at me.

"Do not raise your voice at me! You know I am so glad we never went any further, you are still a pathetic piece of shit and I can't believe I once held you up on a pedestal. You were it for me when I was 16, I thought you had it in you. And then to think how happy I was for Jane, that maybe you really were a great guy, and I was so excited that you would get to have a family with her. Well, you greedy asshole looks like you got two!"

"I'm not going to hurt her." He said as a promise to himself.

"You already have Todd, she just doesn't know it yet."

"I don't know what to say to make you forgive me." I shook my head with sadness and I felt the tears pouring out of my cheek.

" I will never forgive you, nor is it my place to. You better be glad that Jane has a big heart and loves you, because as much as I know it would kill her, I know that you are the only one that can make her happy."

I grabbed my stuff to just get ready at the studio. "This conversation between us never happened Todd. You get your shit together, real soon because I can only avoid her a little longer."

"I got her a ring." He pulled it out of his pant pocket to show me, and I did approve, and I knew Jane would be satisfied with it as well.

"Don't do it under false pretenses. Make sure she knows everything, because if you keep building on these lies, you are going to lose everything."

Chapter Thirty-Four

I left feeling less resolved than I ever had before. As I came down the stairs from my old apartment, I looked across the street to see Jer waiting for me. I am sure that my mascara was running down my face and I could see him steadily walk towards me, with raw emotion on his face.

"I think we need to get away this weekend Iz, you need a break." He said it as if it was gospel. "I can't go." I thought about telling him the truth that I had to fake it with Bo this weekend for Ella's sake, but I couldn't. I knew it would hurt him because he didn't understand my love for that little girl. He would assume that it was just me having issues letting go of Bo, and for that reason alone I decided not to tell him.

"But I do need to go to work this weekend and I would really love it if you would come with me."

"I wish I could, I just have been running so behind lately with editing. I just don't think it will work this weekend, but soon I promise. I want to go home and see everyone!"

"Well everyone will be highly disappointed when I don't come into town waving my sword around and bringing the girl home that I saved from the tower."

"Jer, the city is hardly a tower, and I am hardly a princess. They will understand."

"You're right babe. I think they are used to you not coming home anyway." Even though I knew that he didn't mean it in a malicious way, I felt the jab right in my stomach. I knew that he saw my face, and he gently placed his hand on my side.

"Iz…..I didn't, you know….I just…."
"I get it Jer, it's fine. I should have expected that, just didn't realize how much it would hurt when the words came from you."

"Babe." He whispered, leaning his forehead to mine. "It's fine. I have some errands to run and I probably won't get the chance to see you before you leave town. You'll be back Monday, right?"

"Yes, but you know I can't stay here, forever right?"

I just nodded, because as much as I knew the reality I still wasn't ready to accept it. I felt like I would always crave the city, and the life that I had built here all by myself. I was slowly becoming more aware of my anxiety of leaving the only home I seemed to know anymore.

Jer leaned it for a deep kiss. I felt the warm sensation rush through my body, and I wanted to stay in this moment. In the middle of the craziest city, on a quiet street lined with trees that created a shady archway above us, in this kiss and totally and completely head over heels.

As he pulled away, I felt the urge to cry, and I couldn't decipher if it was out of happiness or sadness. "Don't." He whispered again pulling me into him. "I'll be back in three days, I'm sure you can manage." I nodded slowly, holding myself together, and I watched my love hail a taxi and leave me, on the perfect street, in my favorite place, all alone.

Chapter Thirty-Five

When the taxi turned the corner, I knew that there was only one way to survive the weekend. Work my ass off. It's the only way I knew how to keep my mind on track, to completely overwhelm myself with tasks.

First on the agenda, I called Becca and shouted out about a dozen orders, first on the list was finding me a place to sublet for the next two months to help with my transition. And hopefully move everything in by Monday.

I also needed to shoot a text to Jane to let her know that I will be staying at the plaza this weekend until Jer returns. She texted back immediately: *girls night tonight? I could totally go for some junk food and a bitch fest.*

I smiled and felt the same. *Of course, see you around 7:30.*

I walked into my studio and saw Becca running around like I was the Devil who wears Prada, I glanced down at my yoga pants and oversized off the shoulder t-shirt and laughed.

"Calm down Becca, seriously you are overworking yourself."

"Coming from you, I must look insane right now." Becca knew me very well, and knew that when I was in the zone I was a workaholic.

I turned and looked at my studio, and fell in love with it all over again. The large lights, the vanity for hair and makeup and then I got a great idea.

"Becca what is on my schedule for this weekend?"

"Just a shoot tomorrow morning and you are actually completely free Saturday and Sunday, you had me clear your schedule so you could spend time with Jer remember?" Her voice was shaky, afraid that she possibly misunderstood me.

"That's perfect! Let's keep it that way and see if we can't get ahold of Kevin for hair and makeup Saturday, shouldn't take long!"

"Ok, what's the name of the client? Ella Bronson." I smiled to myself, and began to plan an amazing weekend for Ella.

I grabbed my phone and texted Bo.

This weekend is a go, under one condition. He responded right away.

Thank God. I was getting nervous. Anything babe, you just say the word and I'll make it happen.

Saturday, I want Ella to come to the studio, I am going to have her hair and makeup done as well as a shoot before we go to dinner and a show.

I could hear Becca on the phone confirming that Kevin was available!

Ah my Bells, however am I going to fall out of love with you? More importantly how will I ever be able to make Ella as happy as you do. You're going to be a great mother one day.

That's all he had to say to make my stomach hurt. I tried to ignore the last text and move on with planning this weekend. I had Becca finish arranging everything from the hair and makeup to the wardrobe to be available and 25 outfit changes; to be sure she found something she liked.

I finished up all of my planning, and grabbed the laptop to do some editing at the hotel tonight. I saw that Jer had sent 3 text messages already.

I miss you already.

It's not too late to book a plane ticket.

I love you···to the moon and back.

I called his phone and it went straight to voicemail. "Hey you, have fun this weekend and don't forget to check in on Red for me. See you in 70 hours and 15 minutes! I love you···.to the moon and back."

<u>Chapter Thirty-Six</u>

When Jane came in I had already gotten into the ice cream, and possibly eaten about 13 peanut butter filled Oreos.

"Do Not judge me." I mumbled with ice cream coming out of my mouth. She looked exhausted.

"What happens in the Plaza, stays in the Plaza. Now give me a spoon." I handed her one and laughed as she plopped down on the couch.

"Todd is acting like a weirdo, and honestly I don't have time for it."
She got right to the point, so I decided to get right to mine as well. This is how most of our conversations were. We didn't have time to bullshit each other either.

"I'm spending the weekend with Bo and Ella, Jer doesn't know and went home for the weekend."

"Shit. You win." She laughed as she put another spoonful of ice cream to her mouth. Sadly, I knew that I didn't win, that my problems are somewhat mediocre in comparison to hers. At least she didn't know yet, but I had a gut feeling that by the end of next week, she would be doing all the talking and I would be doing all the listening.

We talked for what seemed like hours, which was only 45 minutes. We discussed the fact that I probably should have told Jer, especially since he knows me better than anyone, and we both knew that I would eventually tell him anyway. I explained to her how I just didn't want to hurt him, and then I became angry with myself because I was being a hypocrite. I had just yelled at Todd for not being forthcoming with Jane, and here I was. Just call me pot···and Todd was most definitely the kettle.

Right before we fell asleep, I sent Jer a quick text. He should have been home by now but I haven't heard from him yet.

Hey. Hope you made it safely. Call me when you get a chance?

I decided that I would tell Jer everything, and ask him his permission, but I know Jer and I know that he would understand. I'm not quite sure why I didn't just tell him in the first place.

Chapter Thirty-Seven

When I woke up, I was excited that I would be seeing Ella in just a few hours. I was also sore from Jane kicking me through the night.

"Good morning sleeping beauty." I nudged her softly.

"Can I just order room service and stay here for a little while?" The baby was sucking the energy right out of her.

"Of course. I have to get going, Bo will be dropping Ella off at the studio in an hour!"

"Call me later and tell me how it went. I can't wait to hear from you….." The last part was interrupted by a yawn, and she was fast asleep as I jumped into the shower.

I realized that I didn't have the dress that I wanted to wear tonight so I quickly called Bo and asked him to bring it. He was beyond nice, and had not stopped calling me Baby, either Ella was standing right there or he was trying to push his luck with me. Regardless, I hurried him off the phone and jumped in the shower.

I decided against wearing any makeup or doing my hair, hoping that Kevin would have also allotted some time for me.

I walked into the studio and saw that Ella was already there. Becca was showing her all the outfits. She turned and saw me and came running into my arms. "Oh. My. Gosh. I don't know how you did all this for me, but I feel like a princess. Thank you. Thank you. Thank you."

I whispered into her ear… "Don't tell anyone but you are a princess." She gave me one last squeeze and then ran over to admire the clothes again. I was waiting until the end of the shoot to tell her that the designers were going to let her keep them.

I felt warmth across my stomach and looked down to Bo's arms wrapped around me. They felt foreign and safe all at the same time. "Bo." I said under my breath.

"Bells, we have a role to play for the next 48 hours. She's a smart girl and she would know something was up if I didn't touch you. You know I couldn't keep my hands off of you."

"Don't press your luck this weekend, I mean it."

"I won't. I'm just glad that Jer is allowing all of this, even though I can't stand him."

I still haven't heard from Jer, and I that pang of guilt that I had buried under the excitement of the weekend was front and center again. I handed Bo my coffee and by the looks of it, he had planned on sticking around for the shoot. I couldn't blame him, I wouldn't pass up an opportunity to see my child so happy either. He looked great wearing a plain black t-shirt and dark jeans. I could see that he was taking his anger out at the gym, his arms were bulging out of his shirt. Knowing Bo, he could have just bought a smaller shirt to make them look bigger.

I sat on the futon playing with my camera while Ella was getting her hair and makeup done. I smiled every time I heard her squeal with excitement.

Bo sat down beside me. "I really can't thank you enough for doing this, especially after I was such a douche bag."

"This⋯" I looked around the room. "Is not for you, this is for that little girl. She has stolen my heart Bo, I could only hope to one day have a daughter just like her." I don't know why I felt the need to confess this to Bo, but by the time I had changed my mind I was already feeling vulnerable.

"Maybe I'll ask her for some tips."

"Tips on what?"

"How to steal your heart⋯.and just a reminder, I can give you a little girl just like that."

I didn't even know how to respond to him, so I just shoved him in a playful manner. That's when he pulled me in and pressed his lips to mine.

The playful shove I had just given him, because a full force punch to the arm.

"Ouch Bells. What the hell?" He rubbed his arm and genuinely looked confused. "Seriously? You are going to ask me what the hell? You know what Bo. This is your last warning, I'm so good at acting I can come down with a stomach bug at any moment and this weekend is over. Do not forget that this is a favor."

"You're right totally uncalled for, but I know you felt it."

"Felt what Bo? You shoving your tongue down my throat?" I was irritated now, more like fuming and he could tell.

"I'm sorry, obviously the feeling isn't mutual."

After two hours of shooting, outfit changes, hair and makeup touch ups, Ella was the happiest little girl and ready to go out for a night on the town. I slipped into my plain black dress and nude heels, and fortunately Kevin did leave enough time to make me look my best.

"Wow, my two favorite ladies look amazing." Bo picked up my camera and started taking pictures of Ella and I. We were having a blast, I had to remind myself that I was pretending and this is not my reality anymore. I squeezed Ella into a hug and stared at her. She looked up at me with such a genuine love, it took everything in me not to cry. I couldn't help but wonder if this was our last weekend together. I heard the shutter go off on my camera, and I knew that the moment Bo just captured would be one I would never forget.

We went out front, and before I could see what was causing the reaction I heard Ella scream. I nearly tripped down the stairs when I turned the corner I felt and instantaneous relief. There was a stretch limo, with a red carpet, this was all too much for me, but for Ella it was more than she could have ever dreamt.

Bo came up behind me. "You know, I think this is a weekend none of us will ever forget. And even though I know you deserve an Emmy for this performance, you have to know that I am not acting a bit of it." I nodded my head and started for the limo.

I checked my phone at least a dozen times on the ride to the restaurant. Still not a word from Jer. I was so worried; I started to get knots in my stomach. Surely, he would have called by now. I sent him another text.

Are you ok? I haven't heard from you at all!!!!!

Bo grabbed my hand, forcing me to put the phone down. Ella was still in awe of the sights of the city.

"I don't think I have ever seen anything so beautiful in my life!" She said staring out at the horse drawn carriages lit up surrounding central park.

Bo whispered in my ear "I know I have."

I knew how Bo worked; he wouldn't stop until he got what he wanted. I'm sure he still figured he had a chance with me, otherwise he wouldn't be laying it on so thick right now.

I just played along in front of Ella, but that was it. I heard the text tone go off on my phone and nearly jumped out of my seat. It was from Jer.

I'm fine. Just been busy with work. Call you tomorrow.

I didn't want to read too much into the text, because I have been known to get myself worked up over nothing but there was something off about his text.

Before I could overthink it we arrived at dinner. The rest of the night went exactly as planned. Dinner was spectacular followed by The Lion King on Broadway, which was one of my favorites. Ella was equally impressed with the show, and she looked to be about exhausted as I was.

I was staring out into space in the limo, with Ella sound asleep on my side.

"Thank you again Bells. You really pulled through for me." Bo was staring at me from across the limo. I was glad that we were distanced because this late at night, after a few drinks he was looking quite delicious. I know that was the alcohol talking so I did my best to keep my mouth shut until it was out of my system.

"When have I ever not pulled through for you Bo?"

"Only when you broke my heart." He glanced down at his lap, refusing to make eye contact.

"Now is not the time to talk about this Bo, and you know it." I said the last words through my teeth.

"I know, but I'll never stop fighting for you." As he said those words, I remember asking Jer to fight for me. What is it with us women? I know what it is, we all want this fairy tale, this picture-perfect relationship where we marry the knight in shining armor, that has to save us from whatever battle we create.

"Bo, there was once a time that was all I wanted. Actually, it is all I want, the only problem is you're not the one I want fighting for me."

"It's ok, I get it. I know he is the one for you, but what happens when you're the one for me?"

The conversation was getting too deep and we were only ten blocks from home when I heard my phone go off. I saw that it was a text from Red, so I quickly opened the text. My phone slid out of my hand when I saw a very pregnant Melissa and Jer at the bar together. Jer's arms were wrapped around her and her head was resting on his shoulder.

"I'm going to be sick." Bo told the driver to stop and I slid Ella over to the other side of the limo. I jumped out of the car, and my entire dinner poured onto the streets of Manhattan.

Bo jumped out behind me, and began to rub my back.

"Was it something you ate?" I just shook my head and began to sob. "Take me home."

"Where do you want me to take you Bells, these days you're somewhat of an orphan." Had I been in a better mood I would have laughed at the last line, because it was so true.

"Take me home with you." Bo scooped me up off of the street and held me in his lap as I cried the last ten blocks.

"Shhhhhh. It's ok, whatever it is it will be ok." I never knew it was possible for Bo to be so comforting. I think he was taken out of his comfort zone in this moment, but I was going to continue to be selfish because right now I needed what he was giving me.

As we pulled up to his apartment I felt like I couldn't even move.

"I'm going to take Ella up, I'll be right back for you. Stay here." I just nodded.

He was gone for what seemed like a second. Which didn't give me enough time to process what I saw from Red's text.

He carried me up the stairs and laid me on the bed. I felt so unlike me, like I was a shell of myself. How could she not be pregnant? And why hasn't he called me! I couldn't even bear to think about it anymore. I needed to shut my mind off.

"Here are some pajamas for you. Did you want to talk about it?" I just shook my head and held my hands up for Bo to slip the dress off. He did so without even pausing for a second. I was wearing a black bra and silk g string.

"Bells······God." He traced the outline of my body with his hand, and I felt it shaking.

"Just hold me." He undid my bra, and immediately put the t-shirt on me. I laid in bed and heard my phone go off again. I saw him pick it up and the look on his face meant that there were more photos that I knew I couldn't bear to see right now.

He placed the phone down and turned it on silent. Bo came right up behind me and wrapped his arms around me, and I realized that at this moment in time, Bo was my knight in shining armor.

Chapter Thirty-Eight

When morning came, I turned to see Ella had joined us in the bed at some point in the night. "Good morning my beautiful ladies." Bo came into the bedroom wearing a loose pair of sweats. I don't know why, but just a plain pair of sweats beat out all the suits he wears on any given day. He handed me a cup of coffee and whispered "You're going to need to drink the whole cup before you check your phone."

"I don't want to check it." I said staring into the cup. I looked up at him. "Has he called?"

I knew that this question was a slap in the face to Bo, but I needed him to answer it. He just shook his head, and I felt the tears stinging my eyes.

"Ella, how about you and I go grab some bagels for breakfast and bring them back here?" She jumped up before he got the whole sentence out.

Thank you I mouthed to him.

"I'll meet you out there in one second baby girl." I could hear her little feet run across the hall floor.

"Listen, I don't know what that fucker is thinking, but I swear to God I'll kick his ass!"

"Don't. Just don't." I said through my tears and shaky voice.

"Whatever you want me to do, whatever you need me to be just let me know."

Bo placed a sweet kiss on my forehead and headed out the door.

I picked up the phone to call Jane. I saw that I had 3 missed calls from Red.

I decided to call him back first, but braced myself for whatever I was going to hear.

"Jesus Izabella, about time you answered that damn phone. What the hell do you have a cell phone for if you never answer it?" Red was mad, and mumbling. Although I didn't know much about my brother I knew that when he got mad he couldn't make sense of anything.

"I'm sorry, I was out. What the hell is going on?"

"Well I don't know what the fuck happened. I was bartending last night and Jer came in, he was with Melissa all night, and totally ignoring the fact that I was staring him down the whole fucking time. Anyway we had words, and I kicked him out of the bar."

"You kicked him out of his own bar?"

"Well I mean, I asked him to leave and told him that he was being blatantly disrespectful and I wasn't having it on my shift."

"Ok, I'm not following Red."

"See here's the thing, I'm not either. All of a sudden Melissa shows up after no one has seen her in a month and she's hanging all over Jer. I mean aren't you guys getting married? What the hell!"

I sat in silence trying to figure out the situation myself.

"And she's totally not pregnant so I don't know, anyway this morning I woke up feeling like an ass because you know I kicked him out of his own bar, I mean maybe he was just being nice. So, I went over to apologize this morning."

I could hear his voice start to shake. My poor baby brother, fighting my battles for me.

"Anyway, please don't be mad at me."

"I'm not mad at you, just spit it out."

"I went to his house and Melissa answered the door. She was wearing his fucking shirt! So when she called him to come to the door I didn't ask any questions, I just punched him in the face and left."

Ok, now I was speechless. I had no idea what to say, and I felt the walls crashing down around me.

"I have to go." I hung up the phone and it started ringing again. I answered and yelled " I said I have to go!"

"Iz?" Jers voice came through the other line. "Don't hang up. Fuck, I fucked up Iz. I'm so fucking sorry." That's all I had to hear. I hung up the phone and called Jane. I explained to her everything that had happened and everything that I knew, which once I laid it all on the table didn't seem like much.

"Do you think I am over reacting? Jane I am freaking out."

"No, you aren't overreacting, I'm going to cut his balls off. I'm on my way over you're at the hotel, right?"

"Uhh, no I'm at Bo's."

"I'm totally not judging you right now, on my way over. "

I went into the bathroom, and fortunately my toothbrush and some make up was still in my drawer. I pulled myself together and had to make it through the next two hours until Lauren came to get Ella.

I heard Ella storm through the door. "We got your favorite kind Bells!!!!"

I took a deep breath in and met her in the kitchen.

"Well aren't you just the sweetest!" I pulled her in for a deep hug, that was more for me than her.

We spent the rest of the morning eating and playing dance central. Jane arrived shortly after breakfast and sat on the couch and watched as we played on the wii.

"I wish I could burn calories watching you." She would mumble every other dance.

The two hours had flown by and Lauren was at the door ready to pick up Ella.

As Ella came in for one last hug, I heard her crying, and in turn I matched her tear for tear.

"I'm just going to miss you so much Bells. You made me feel like a real princess this weekend."

"Don't forget Ella, you are a real princess!" I kissed the top of her head and sent her out the door to her mom.

"Oh, Lauren I almost forgot I am having all the clothes from the shoot yesterday sent to your house if that's ok."

"Izabella, I never thought I would be ok with Bo being in her life, let alone one of his well you know. But I am so glad that it's you, she loves you she really does. I couldn't ask for anything more. Thank you."

      With that I shut the door and collapsed to the floor.

Chapter Thirty-Nine

I wasn't sure if I passed out, or if I just checked out of reality, regardless I woke up to Jane wiping my face with a wet towel.

"I'm fine. I'm fine." I shouted, startling Jane and Bo.

"Bo, take her to the bed." He was afraid of Jane and didn't blink before scooping me up and taking me to the bed.

"Bells, we need to talk. Jer called me about ten minutes ago."

"I don't want to hear it, Jane, how can he possibly?" She knew how I felt.

"I know, I know. Let's not talk about it right now." She glared at Bo.

"Get us take out, you know the drill." He picked up the phone and started dialing, it made me chuckle a little bit because he was on edge, a rare sight to see.

I decided to turn my phone off, and lie in Bo's bed with Jane for the remainder of the day and watch chick flicks. I missed the days that we shared like this, back when life was as simple as finding the right dress for a night out. My life has become somewhat of a cluster fuck in the last year.

After 6 hours of Sunday laziness, tears and laughter with Bo and Jane I decided that I needed to face reality and figure out exactly what transpired over the weekend.

I wasn't sure whom I should call first, so as I picked up the phone I was surprised to see myself calling my Mother.

"Mom?" The phone was silent.

"Oh baby, Red told me what happened. I don't even know what to say. Actually, I do know what to say. Jer is a little shit!" I chuckled at my Mom, and felt comforted by her voice even though I knew her embrace was at least 400 miles away.

"I Just don't know what happened mom, none of it makes sense!"

"I couldn't agree with you more; this little tramp shows up out of nowhere and is fixin' to steal that man of yours! Worst of all he let it happen."

"Ma, you are hearing one side of the story." I kept trying to remind myself of the same thing.

"Well you sound way to calm to me, I almost punched him myself when I found out, thankfully Red beat me to it."

Although I was getting no answers from my Ma, it made me calmer and ready to deal with the real issues.

"I've got to call him Mom. I have to hear it from him."

"Well we all have our battles. You call me if you need me. I love you."

"Love you too."

I sat on the couch and had Jer's number pulled up for at least 10 minutes.

"Don't call him." Bo sat down beside me, I turned and saw Jane fast asleep on the bed.

He brushed the hair out of my eyes. "Don't call him. Let me be your knight, let me protect you from this pain."

"Bo, I have to know what happened." I rested my head on his chest.

He wrapped his arms around me. "Whatever he says, whatever happens, I'll still fight for you." I nodded into his chest.

"I'll give you some privacy. I'm going for a run. I'll be back in 30 minutes, but I have my phone. If you need me."

"I know, I'll call." I finished his sentence for him.

I grabbed a blanket and wrapped myself up in it and pressed the call button. I could feel every nerve in my body shaking.

"Thank God you called back." The phone only rang once.

"Jer, I don't⋯I don't even know what to say." I started sobbing and he could hear it.

"I'm so sorry Iz, I never meant to hurt you. I didn't hurt you⋯fuck I don't even know what I am saying right now."

"Start with what the hell you were doing with Melissa! And why isn't she pregnant."

"Well, that's not really my story to tell."
"Jer so help me, if you ever want to see me again⋯." Anger was the only emotion I was wearing now.

"Ok so Melissa called me on the way down and asked me to meet her at Dr. Unks when I got into town."

"How did she know you were coming to town?" I was livid.
"I told her. I asked her how she was doing, I mean fuck Iz, Todd is a dick you know it!"

"I never said I had a problem with you talking to her Jer, the problem is that you have not once called me. The whole time you were with her I was worried sick about you."

"I know I fucked up, but nothing happened I swear. She lost the baby last month. She asked if I would meet her for drinks, she's been having a really hard time dealing with the whole thing. She doesn't have anyone!"

"I don't know why you are raising your voice with me, you are the one that slept with another woman!"

"Iz, baby. I didn't sleep with her. I would never, you know that you're it for me and I am so sorry if I ever made you question it. You should know how I feel, that will never change, no woman will ever change what I feel about you."

"Why didn't you call me? Why was it some big secret?"
"I knew you would act like this!" Yelling again.

"Act like what Jer? Concerned? Pissed? Heartbroken? Devastated? You pick because right now I am all of them."

I heard the door slam shut. "Bells are you ok?" Fuck Bo!
I knew that Jer heard him. "Iz, where are you right now?" Fuck. Fuck. Fuck.
"I'm at Bo's."
"Fuck you!" And then the line went dead.

Chapter Forty

Bo came around the corner just as I threw my phone against the wall and it shattered. "Bells." He came over and sat beside me, he didn't put his arms around me, maybe because he wasn't trying to push his luck, or maybe because he was trying to protect himself.

I didn't want to pull Bo back into all of this drama, because as of right now I had no clue where I stood.

He got up and walked over to my phone to collect the pieces that were remaining. "Well I don't think you'll be getting any calls soon."

I looked at him, and saw pain in his eyes. "What's wrong Bo?"

"Nothing, why?" he turned so I couldn't see his face.

"You're lying! Please don't lie to me, I swear I can't take one more lie in my life right now."

He turned and I saw his face reddened with anger. "I just hate him ok? I can't stand what he is doing to you! I've done many fucked up things Bells, but not once would I ever…would I even think about….."

"It's ok. I know." I patted my hand on the couch. I think that for the first time Bo was realizing the pain that he caused me in the months before, the night that he found me on his doorsteps.

"I'm sorry if I have ever made you feel this way."

I just nodded in agreement, afraid of what would come out of my mouth. I was vulnerable with Bo right now, and as tempting as he was I still belonged to Jer.

I put my arms around his waist and pulled him in close. I don't know how I got to this place in my life, where the man in front of me is finally who I have been waiting for all my life. And the man I always pictured behind me was coming up just short of what I needed.

"Is it ok if I stay here until Monday? Becca is supposed to be finding me a place by then."

"You know that this is still your home, you can always come here."

I went to check on Jane, and admired her ability to sleep through everything that had occurred. I crawled into bed with her, and drifted off to sleep.

I was woken two hours later by Jane's cackling laugh and the sound of pots and pans in the kitchen. I jumped up to investigate, wiping the drool from my mouth, and hoping that no one saw it.

As I came into the kitchen I saw Bo, Todd, and Jane laughing hysterically.

"What are you all laughing at?" I had my hands on my hips, doing my best pouty face.

"The pictures that Jane got of you with drool all over your face!" Todd said in between laughs.

I started laughing with them grabbing the phone out of her hands. The pictures were hilarious, as long as they didn't hit the internet I would be fine with it.

"What's for dinner?" I peeked into the pot and before anyone could reply I turned and jumped into Bo's arms! "Chili!!!! It's my favorite."

"I know baby girl, that's why I made it." Had Bo always been this thoughtful?

I decided I was going to keep pretending that nothing happened, until I could wrap my head around what happened anyway.

"I'm thinking that we need a rematch for Just Dance!" I pointed at Bo. He nodded his head and took a sip of his beer.

"Ah but first beer run! Jane, are you coming with me?" She glared over at me, and I forgot that she couldn't drink.

"What pregnant women can still go into the beer store, no?" I rubbed my hand across her belly. She agreed to go with me, but said that I owed her. I mean realistically we always owe one another something, and over the years it just evens out.

On the way to the store she did a great job at not bringing anything up. But when we left, I knew it wouldn't be much longer before she had word vomit.

"Ugh! Fine, I'll be the first one to talk about it." She started, and I couldn't help but laugh at her.

"What the hell is going on? It's like in the matter of one day your life turns to shit how does that happen? And did he cheat on you or not?"

"First, I don't know how that can happen. I really haven't taken the time to process everything. I really don't know if he cheated on me, we never got the chance to talk about it because he found out I was at Bo's."

"Oh, shit." I nod in agreement.

"What's next?" I wasn't sure, and I didn't want to commit to a decision just yet.

"Next is drinking and just dancing." She wrapped her arm in mine and we walked the last block to Bo's.

The night flew by, and for a few hours I was transported to a few months ago, sitting in my apartment with Bo, playing video games and laughing on a Saturday night. It seemed that ever since Jer came back into my life I hadn't had a moment to myself, a moment to laugh and be silly.

I missed having that with Jer before, when he would come up on weekends and we could just be friends that had no true commitment other than to make each other laugh.

The night ended before I was ready for it to, and Jane and Todd were going home. I briefly thought about how Melissa not being pregnant factored into their relationship now, and if Todd would even tell her.

"Well, are you exhausted yet? You've had quite the day."

"Nope. I'm not exhausted, and I am not ready for bed either! Will you do something for me?"

"Anything baby." I would normally correct him calling me this, but right now I didn't have it in me.

"Take me dancing!" He pulled me into him.
"Chili and dancing all in the same night?"
"It would make me feel like a princess." I
whined.
"Baby, how many times do I have to tell you, you
are a princess." I felt the tears stinging my eyes
and ran in the room to get changed.

Within 30 minutes we were on our way into
one of my favorite dance clubs. The alcohol was
quickly absorbing all of my problems, as I danced
the night away. Bo called us a driver to take us
back to the apartment, and I couldn't have been
happier.

Besides the fact that my legs were killing
me from all of the dancing, I also found myself too
intoxicated to do anything except put puke and
sleep. I was fairly confident that I could hold the
throw up until we got to the apartment though.

I woke up from what felt like a coma in Bo's
bed. "Hey. When did we get home?" He was
getting on his suit so I assumed he had to work,
and that Monday was already here.

"Listen lady, I'm no spring chicken
anymore. I can't keep up with you. Serves me right
for falling for a younger girl."

"I don't remember the ride home at all. Did I
throw up?"
He threw his head back and laughed. "All night
long. I wish I had that kind of amnesia."

"Was I gross?" I still felt comfortable with
Bo, and this wasn't the first time that he had seen
me wasted.

"You were fine. Listen I have a long day
ahead of me, if you're still around maybe we can
do dinner?" I heard the sadness in his voice.

"I'll still be here." I knew I wasn't going
anywhere fast that's for sure.

I found myself in the kitchen making
breakfast, when I heard the banging on the door.
"For the love." I mumbled···.

I swung the door open and saw Jer looking
exhausted, and still bruised where Red nailed him
in the jaw. *Serves him right.*

"What Jer, what could you possibly want?"
"We need to talk. Not here." He just pointed outside. I grabbed a sweater, unfortunately in poor taste it was one of Bo's but it would have to work for now.

I felt the wind grab ahold of my skin the second I walked out the door. Jer was wearing a baseball cap, sweats and a plain white t-shirt. He was fumbling with the keys he held in his hands and I knew he was nervous. My head was throbbing and I was tempted to just rain check this conversation for another day, but I had to know.

"Start talking." I was short and firm with my directions.
"Listen, I don't know where you want me to start. I already told you I didn't sleep with her this weekend. I told you she just needed some comfort."

"Why did she sleep at your house?"
"Because she has nowhere else to go." He reached out and the warmth that I expected from his touch was suddenly cold. I just couldn't seem to wrap my head around the whole situation. I felt that I had all the corner pieces, the outline to my puzzle but I was missing the center. The most important piece was missing, and I knew that he was hiding it from me.

The warmth I had expected from Jer was suddenly on my shoulders, but Jer was too far away for me to feel him, both physically and emotionally.

I turned and saw Bo hunched over and out of breath, which was completely out of the ordinary since the only time I have seen him sweat was in his workout clothes.

"Where have you been?" he huffed, still catching his breath. "What's wrong with you, I've been here the whole time! And why are you out of breath? Couldn't afford the cab fare." I joked, because I was honestly nervous.

"I've···we've been trying to call you. And I needed to get to you as fast as I could." I bent down and looked into his eyes.

"Jane is in the hospital. I don't know much, but the baby is coming."
I felt sick. My heart started racing and I just stared at Bo unaware of what to do.
"I'll hail a cab and get into something decent. Save that sweater to snuggle me in later." He winked in Jer's direction. I wasn't sure if he was trying to get Jer pissed, or invite me to stay with him. Jer went to reach for my hand as I turned to go inside. I was glad that Bo had given me directions because in my flustered state I felt like I couldn't function without them.

"Iz let me come with you, I'll take you to the hospital. We can talk there."
"No Jer. JUST GO." I remembered him telling him that he wouldn't leave unless I asked him to. I wasn't sure if he would really go, but my heart felt content if he did.

I ran up the stairs and in a hurried blur got dressed in something halfway presentable, but definitely not an outfit I would document in any capacity. I came out of the room and Bo was nervously looking for my phone, by flipping the seat cushions in every direction.

"I have it right here." I held it up to show him. "Oh, ok perfect. We should get going. I already hailed a cab, is it ok if I go with you." I knew that Bo had run over fifteen blocks to get to me, and yet here he was still asking permission.

"Of course, Bo." I put my hand in his and followed him down the stairs.
The cab ride seemed like the longest I had ever had. "You always do that when you are nervous. Fidget with your hands. It's going to be ok Bells." I just nodded, praying that he was right. "She's really early. Do you know what happened?"

"Todd called me after he tried you and couldn't reach you. Her water broke. Not sure much else."

The rest of the ride was quiet. Bo put his hands-on top of my fidgeting ones to try to calm me. My nerves were beyond the point of that, but it still felt nice to have his support. As we approached the hospital my anxiety reached a new level, even for me. I turned to Bo as he reached for my hand to pull me out of the cab.

"I don't know if I can go in there Bo. I am so scared."

He pulled me into him. I felt his hand behind my head and I could feel his breath on my lips. "You are the strongest woman I know. Jane needs you to be strong for her. I'm not leaving you so you have back up. I'll never leave you."

I suddenly had a burst of confidence. I pulled myself together and marched into the lobby. I kindly asked them to point me in the direction of Jane, which they did. I took a deep breath in convincing myself that I didn't watch Grey's Anatomy every Thursday night for nothing.

I opened the door to her room, with Bo right behind me.

She was sitting up in the bed looking as calm as possible. Nothing like the exorcist I predicted.

"Seriously?" I asked her with a crooked smile. "I know I totally ruined our plans for dinner tomorrow. Lame right?" Her eyes sparkled like the diamond on her finger.

I grabbed her hand. "When?!" She looked over at Todd asleep in the corner of the room. "Right before my water broke."

Just as the story was getting good I was interrupted by Bo handing me a coffee. I nodded to thank him and took a sip. To my surprise when I was expecting the warmth of coffee to brush my lips, I was delighted to have the cool taste of alcohol.

Bo leaned down "don't make it obvious, I had to sneak that contraband in here. Ah the things I do for you."

I took another sip and winked at him, and loved the response of laughter that poured out of his mouth. The nurse walked in with a stern look on her face, and for one second, I thought we had been busted. I glanced over to Bo who held his finger up to his lips.

"Jane, sweetie we are going to prep you for surgery." The nurse said the words calmly, but by the amount of staff that followed in after she delivered the news I felt overtaken by concern.

Bo instinctively grabbed my hand as if the nurse was telling me the news directly. I squeezed his hand and let go, I pushed past Todd who was now standing next to Jane, his face paled in comparison to the natural olive skin that normally glowed when he walked into a room.

Jane looked over at me "It's ok, go wait with Bo. Todd will be with me, I'll be fine." I found myself a little hurt that she didn't want me with her, yet a little happy that it was Todd who was taking my place.

I kissed her forehead and then found myself carefully placed under Bo's broad arms, being escorted to the waiting room.

"I feel like it's been 10 hours." I crossed my arms over my chest. "Bells, it's been twenty minutes." I found the vending machine, and decided to eat my emotions. They came in the form of Reese's, Snickers and chips. I looked at Bo and started laughing.

"What's so funny?" He smirked to the side. "I was just thinking that my choices of guilty pleasures are a lot like you. "Hmmm how's that?"

"Oh, you know···a lot of sweet with just a touch of salt."
He kissed my forehead, "Sounds about right. Does that make me one of your guilty pleasures?"

"My favorite one." I shocked myself with my response. "I like the sound of that, maybe later I will let you indulge." I felt like right now it was taking everything in me not to leave with him.

An hour passed, when the nurse came out and told us that Jane had a baby girl. They were both doing well but the baby was in the NICU. I was beyond relieved to hear that they both made it. I was sure how serious the situations could be, but I knew that I had just received a miracle.

"We will only be able to let one person back to be with her in PACU, Dad is with a baby so would one of you like to join Jane?" Bo nudged me out of shock and I followed behind the nurse with tears brimming in my eyes. I looked back at Bo.

"See ya at home kid." He had his jacket over his arm, and looked utterly exhausted. I took note to remind myself to thank him later, I am sure he was going to spend the rest of the evening working from home, trying to catch up on the day he missed to be there for me.

I hated the feeling of being in a hospital, the white walls, the smell, and the lack of heat gave me chills. I rubbed my arms, but couldn't tell if it was from my anxiety or the actual chill I was feeling.

I pushed through the doors and saw Jane eating ice chips in bed. She looked as normal as she had gone into surgery. "You look amazing Jane!!!"

She gave me a glare "why wouldn't I?" Glad to see that nothing changed. My worry for her was now diminished, and completely transferred to the baby.

"How is she?" I grabbed her hand. "She's amazing. God. I just···I can't believe I am a mom."

"The best one." I couldn't wait to get my hands on that little nugget, but I knew that Jane needed me right now, whether she would ever admit it was another question.

"Where did Bo go?" I told her everything that happened just before I came to the hospital. Including Jer not breathing a word about Melissa, or his affiliation with her.

"Do you think he cheated on you Bells?" When she asked that question I shook my head no. But I asked myself if I really believed that. She was beautiful; smart, not to mention her amazing body. I had nothing on her, and I really felt like I didn't know the whole story about them since the beginning. Maybe I had just been in the dark so long that I had no idea what the light even looked like.

"You probably won't be able to see her until the morning, and they won't let you stay the night." I knew what she was doing, pushing me right into Bo's arms. But seeing her with the lines going into her gown, it wouldn't be fair if I protested.

Chapter Forty-One

Have you ever had that feeling where you just weren't sure where you belong? I felt that with my whole being, completely unsure of almost every aspect in my life except for one. Photography was my outlet, so when I began hailing a cab to my studio instead of Bo's that was the only thing that made sense to me. It was the only place that I belonged, that accepted me for who I was, and even I wasn't sure of that answer.

As I opened the doors I knew exactly what I was going to do. In the dark of my studio I began to undress and set my auto timer on the camera. I wanted to be able to capture myself completely. I had done the shoot for some many others and saw how gratifying it was, I wondered if maybe I would feel the same at the end of the session.

An hour had passed, and within that time I heard my phone ring over ten times. As soon as I heard the sound of the last shutter I walked over to my purse, reached my hand in and turned the phone to silent.

I began uploading my pictures to the computer, and shocked myself at how beautiful they had turned out. In most of the pictures you could only make out the silhouette of my body. The light behind me shined all around the curves of my body and through the slivers of separation in my hair. I opened Photoshop and was caught off guard by the sound of the door opening. I thought for sure I had locked it.

I searched in the darkness for some sort of weapon to protect myself, and started to panic knowing that I had none. I could hear my father now *I've been telling here for years to get her permit, nothing wrong with a pretty girl packing heat.* I should have listened to him.

I looked down at myself completely naked, and another flash of worry crossed my mind. I was basically asking the intruder to rape and kill me. *Great.*

I backed into the corner and I heard Bo quietly whisper my name. I forgot that I had given him a key, and I felt my body shake as the adrenaline pumped through my veins. I came out of the corner and jumped on him, so thankful that I wasn't going to be chopped up into little pieces.

"Is Jer here?"

"No, why?" He looked me up and down, and I became aware again that I was completely nude. I started laughing as I searched in the dark for any article of clothing. Bo handed me his blazer and I threw it on barely covering my breasts.

Bo was scrolling on the computer in my pictures. I almost reached over to stop him, but I knew that at this point in our journey, whatever that may be he would see them eventually anyway.

"Bells⋯..wow. These are incredible. How did you do this?" It warmed my heart to hear him say those things, because I knew he wasn't lying. Bo was always good for an honest opinion on my work.

"I just kind of let the camera capture me. Everything I feel, everything I want to see in myself." I knew that was deep for a couple of photographs but I felt it to be the only accurate description.

He started towards me and pressed his chest against mine. The blazer opened, and I could feel the warmth from his skin press against mine. In almost complete darkness I could see him in a way I never had before.

Bo rested his forehead against mine. I felt his hand reach under the blazer and caress my lower back. I felt my body begging him to go further, and I thought for a moment that we would forever be stuck in this purgatory. Then it happened.

In the darkness and without any warning I felt his lips softly press into mine, and granting him permission I allowed my tongue to slowly enter his mouth.

I didn't want to talk about it, and I didn't want to over think what was happening between us. I knew that Bo had a fear that shook him to the core, and that was more so the reason he wasn't talking. He had been fighting for me for so long, and so hard that he was afraid I would confirm his defeat. It was in the moment where I found us naked on the floor of my studio, about to take the final plunge that I knew I was always his. It took us so long to get to this place, where we were both ready. Both willing to accept each other's pasts that we could finally make a future.

I smiled at him staring down at his chiseled face. He had the facial structure of a Greek God, and the body of a Spartan. He was beyond my expectations for any human, and the most beautiful person I had ever laid my eyes on.

"What are you smiling at, princess?" He flipped me onto my back and rubbed my jaw with his thumb and then slowly caressed it over my lips.

"You. Always you." As the words came out of my mouth he knew what they meant because the second I said them, I could see the surprise on his face. The joy in his eyes, and then I felt him press inside of me.

Every ounce of me that thought I was cheating on Jer vanished, in fact I felt bad because it seems I may have gotten it backwards, this whole time I was cheating on Bo.

As I felt him enter me over and over again I felt complete happiness, content with my world, like nothing could bring me down.

After what seemed like hours I looked over to a sleeping Bo covered only by the blazer. I let out a small laugh, which was big enough to wake him.

"Hey there gorgeous." He wrapped me back up in his arms.

"So I just have to come out and ask it. Because I need to know, I need to be sure that this is what you want. You know I come with baggage and you know that I'm not perfect. But I swear to God Bells, I feel like I could take care of you. I have never in my entire life pictured myself being so wrapped up in a woman. Literally and metaphorically right now." His laughter interrupted himself.

"It's just. I don't know. I don't know how to say it, or what exactly to say to make you understand. I would fight until the end for you. You're it for me, for my whole life I've waited for you, and when you were right in front of me all along I guess I was just waiting for myself to catch up. But I am finally here, and I swear I'm not going anywhere."

"Bo. It will always be you." I felt like I couldn't top what he just said, or match it for that matter. Because no words could ever explain to him the way I fell in love with a man I had been with for so long. I didn't even know that it was possible to feel like I had just met him for the first time.

Bo and I spent the night in the studio, which later included another silhouette shoot of the two of us, which I didn't tell him about or show him for that matter. But they turned out even more spectacular than I have ever imagined.

Chapter Forty-Two

Two months had passed, and it was finally Jane's big day. She made Todd wait until she was back down to a size 4 before she would marry him. At least in front of hundreds of guests. Bo and I were the only two who actually knew that they got married the week she was released from the hospital.

The dressing room was chaotic and I found my zen in Baby B. She looked so much like Jane, except for the fact that unlike her mother she was still filled with pure innocence. Jane finally had her minions zip her dress, she flew in almost all of her cousins for the wedding, which was fine with me since she was nothing short of a bridezilla.

"Gosh Bella, turn that ring around or something you're blinding me over here! What are you trying to steal my spotlight?"

I flipped my ring finger at her, insinuating that I was flipping her the bird. The girls ran over and ogled over my ring. Bo had done a fantastic job picking out the second ring that finally landed a forever place on my finger.

"Is it real?" The youngest cousin said as she looked up at me in disbelief. I shook my head. It wasn't the size of the ring that I think threw everyone off was the clarity. Bo had searched hard and long for a flawless ring and even used that in his proposal speech.

"Bells, tell them about the proposal! Ugh it's my favorite and it will get them out of my hair for awhile." She laughed at her pun because the hairdresser had just started styling her hair.

"Well, ladies." I could see the excitement on their face as I started the story. I felt like a kindergarten teacher about to start story time.

I told them the whole story and even drew some parts out because I knew that Jane was feeling a little overwhelmed.

The day really was magically and the proposal may have been a little cliché for some, but to me it was perfect. A month ago, Bo and I had spent the entire day walking around central park, visiting all of my favorite stops. At the end, just as it started getting dark the Cinderella style carriages lined up the perimeter of the park. "Have you ever been in a carriage?" He asked, and I shook my head no.

"Well every princess should ride in a horse drawn carriage at least once in her life." He led me into the carriage, once I stepped in I felt him gone from behind me. When I turned to look for him he was on one knee.

"Bells, I know that our story has had its flaws. We've faced villains, shattered dreams, and pain. But we've also seen miracles, magic and love. Please let me give you the fairy tale ending; let me treat you like the princess you are. Let me be your prince. Marry me?"

The girls were so giddy, I felt bad for their future husbands they had a lot to live up to.

"Just kidding girls!" I laughed at myself for even coming up with that story.

"Tell them the real story Bells." Jane called out from the other side of the room.

"Alright. Alright. A week after Bo and I decided to get back together he came home one night from work. I had just finished making dinner for us." I omitted the part that I was only wearing an apron.

"I sat down to eat and Bo came around to the side of the table when I looked up he was on one knee. He told me that he couldn't stand one more second of me not being his wife. Instead of a box he handed me an envelope, with two tickets to the Bahamas inside."

"The rest is history girls! We got on the plane twenty minutes later and within two days were husband and wife." What I didn't fill them in on was the part where Bo surprised me and had all of my immediate family already there. Or about the letter he gave me just before we got married. I remembered it word for word.

My Dearest Bells,

I can't begin to tell you

Jane gave me a thank you glance, and I could tell that she was starting to get nervous. She stood up and turned around, and even put me in awe. She had a strapless lace v neck gown, that dipped low in the back coming into a V just above her panty line. I knew I could never pull off half of the things that she wore, but this outfit was especially made for her.

"You ready lady?" She nodded and took a deep breath.

"I'll see you out there." I hugged her and picked up baby B, who was all decked out in a dress almost as gorgeous as her Mother's.

I walked down the aisle, which was nothing but white rose petals, down to the archway made of gardenias. The vineyard that they had chosen for their venue was stunning, and I was a little jealous that I would never be able to compete with this wedding.

I looked over at Todd, who cleaned up better than I could have ever imagined, and right next to him stood Bo. When I made it to the end Bo winked and smiled at me, which I am sure made every other girl jealous.

The ceremony was amazing, and the tears flowed, even though I gave Jane my word I would keep it together.

I watched Jane and Todd take their first dance as husband and wife, while Bo sat beside me with his hand in mine. We technically hadn't had our own first dance yet, since we were married on the island so we were patiently waiting to see what our song would be.

I looked at the tears on Jane's face, which mirrored mine. I would have never in a million years guessed that I would be at a wedding for these two. I was also surprised that I really didn't know that much about their relationship. How exactly they worked, what made them click. I know that the string that ties everything together was baby B, and I was happy that she would have such amazing parents.

An hour passed before another slow song came on, and it was perfectly fitting for Bo and I, and although at times I thought it to be quite cliché in this moment it was made for us.

He found me through the crowd and pulled me into him as we danced to At Last by Etta James. "Can you believe we are here?" He said as he stared me in the eyes.

"You mean at Todd and Jane's wedding?" I smirked at him knowing that he was referring to us being married.

"You're a brat you know that right?" He leaned down and kissed my forehead.

The entire evening flew by, and at the end we practically held a riot to have the DJ continue to play for another hour. Bo even offers to pay him double.

Fortunately for me, he wouldn't agree to the bidding. I was exhausted, and wanted nothing more than to get home in our bed.

I kissed Jane and Todd goodbye, and knew that I would see them in the morning. Todd's parents were going to keep baby B so they could spend their wedding night alone. I was sure to get text messages throughout the night from her for me to check on the baby.

Finally, with my shoes in my hands, and Bo's jacket around my shoulders we got into the limo. My hair, which was once, and updo was now a mess of curls that poured over my shoulders.

"We'll be finding bobby pins for weeks…sorry." I shrugged my shoulders at Bo. "You act like this would be something new." I was pressed up against him in the back of the limo staring out into the city, the lights were so bright it hardly seemed possible for it to be the middle of the night.

Bo leaned his head on my shoulder and I could hear the soft snore escaping his mouth. His phone was buzzing in his pocket and through the buzz that he was currently in I knew that he wouldn't feel me slide it out of his pocket.

I saw the name appear across the screen, and felt flashbacks from the months before when I found out that Jane had been talking to him behind my back. I swiped my finger across the phone, and heard his voice without the phone being held up to my ear. I closed my eyes tightly and ended the call.

As much as my curiosity wanted to further explore Bo's call log, I shut his phone off and slid it back into his pocket.

I contemplated asking Bo if he had talked to Jer before, how many times, what was the reason, but none of the answers would satisfy me. I nudged Bo awake when we pulled up in front of our apartment.

"How long have I been asleep? I drooled on your shoulder, sorry." I laughed thinking how many girls would have this man drooling all over them. I grabbed a piece of his shirt and put it to his face to wipe the rest of it off.

"What would I do without you, beautiful girl?"

"You'd be a slobbering mess that's for sure." We climbed the stairs to our apartment; I opened the door to the wonderful familiar scent of our home. It smelled of cinnamon like my mother's cooking, mixed with holidays yet also had the calming soft scent of chamomile.

"When are we going to open these?" I snatched the red envelopes out of his hands. Bo got the first five and wasn't sure he should tell me. They come in regularly every Monday. As badly as I want to know what is inside of them, I know that there may be a truth that I am not ready to know. Something that would make me feel guilty, and placing the blame on him is what helped me get through my blissful days on marriage with Bo.

"WE are not opening anything. I may open them···eventually." He dropped them down, and let out a heavy sigh, I was sure that he was just as curious as I was about the contents.

The way that things ended with Jer, I assumed that the first letter was built from anger. I should probably toss that one out, and the others probably still had some remnants of hostility subtly throughout them. I figured if I would ever sit down and read them I would start with the last one. That one would surely put a smile on my face, rather than bringing the tears to the surface.

"When are you going to start packing?" Bo had the suitcase next to the bed for the past three days; I have been completely avoiding it. Since we decided to elope, my parents thought it was only fair that we had a small reception in my hometown. I couldn't argue with them, because truthfully, they were right, and they were paying for the whole thing.

"I'm going to knock it out tonight, that will give me one day to think over all the things that I will second guess." I always preferred waiting until the last minute to pack, but not because I'm a procrastinator, but because I would worry for an entire week and end up repacking five times anyway.

Bo made his way into the shower, which gave me the perfect opportunity to hack into his phone. I went through his call logs, and saw that the call from Jer tonight had been the first in at least a week.

I ran so many scenarios through my head for the purpose behind his call. Could he be in trouble? Why would he call Bo of all people if that were the case? Maybe he wanted to ask about me, but then again, I am sure that he got word of my wedding.

I decided that very moment was the time that I needed to start packing. Most of the clothes that made their way into my suitcase were casual with the exception of the two outfits that were options for the reception. Jane would be heading down a day after us, so I was more at ease about forgetting something.

Bo decided that we should fly down rather than drive this time. I figured he may have thought about pulling his hair out after spending 13 hours in a car with me. Not that he hasn't done it before, but I think it would be more pleasurable for both of us if we just flew.

I also know that Bo did it to make me happy, because he has a top-secret fear of flying. He had to fly a lot for work and would never admit it to coworkers or anyone for that matter.

I only discovered this fear when we boarded the plane for the Bahamas, and saw his leg trembling. Once I asked him, it took half a flight of denial before I was able to get him to admit to the fear, one that he kept hidden from childhood.

I often find it's the little things that I know about him, that no one else knows that make me feel so special. Like I am a part of a top-secret organization, and the knowledge I gain is to remain confidential.

I had half of my suitcase filled and decided to call it quits. I lay on the bed and reached into my nightstand drawer. I heard the water still running so I knew I was safe.

I picked up the test and stared at the two pink lines one more time. I had only known for two days, but for those two days I decided not to tell anyone. I was pretty good at this top-secret stuff. I wanted to tell Bo so badly but I just wasn't sure how.

I couldn't take my eyes off of the test as my hand subconsciously went to rest on my stomach.

"Bells···" I looked up to a Bo wrapped in nothing but a towel with his skin glistened with small beads of left over water. The towel dropped to the ground and I had a naked, glistening Bo on top of me.

I quickly slid the stick back into the drawer without Bo catching a glimpse. We were still in the honeymoon phase of our marriage, but I couldn't imagine ever being able to resist him again. My attraction to his was so much deeper than his impeccable body, or his deep seductive voice. There were often moments where I would quietly watch him doing such a simple task, like folding the laundry, or dancing around the bedroom in his underwear that would make me feel like a teenage girl again.

We would be getting home a day before the reception, and Lauren was going to come on the day of the celebration and bring Ella. She had been so wonderful about letting her visits become more regular. I couldn't wait to tell Bo that he would get the chance to be a parent for all of those years that he missed before.

Chapter Forty-Three

We boarded the plane and Bo squeezed my hand immediately after buckling us both in. I wished that I could transfer his anxiety to myself. I loved flying, and wished that I had more opportunities to travel for work. I thought about expanding my business to other locations, and upping my prices but my schedule left little time.

The flight went so quickly it was barely enjoyable for me. I had a lot on my mind, and still hadn't thought of the perfect idea to tell Bo he was going to be a Dad.

It was killing me not to just spit it out, and I almost did halfway through our flight.

When we arrived at the airport Red and a very pregnant Jess were waiting for us at the gate. She was due any day, and looked positively wonderful, although she swore she looked like a whale. I needed to remember this from my perspective now when I am 9 months pregnant.

"Hey Sis, glad you guys made it safely!" Even though it had been forever since I felt my brother's arms around me, it was so familiar. I rubbed Jess's belly "Oh Gosh I am so sorry I didn't ask. Is it ok if I touch your belly?" I remember Jane giving people nasty looks when they tried to touch her. "Izabella, this is your niece of course you can rub my belly!" She was so sweet, I was really happy for Red that he had her.

"How's the bar going?" Bo put out his hand to shake Reds. "Good man thanks for asking." Red pulled him into a man hug. "Oh, and welcome to the family bro."

I was so happy to see my brother being genuinely nice to Bo, and acting like such a man.

"When did you grow up, Brat?" I gave him a playful shove. "When you stopped being a bitch." He taunted back at me. "So then shall we call you Peter Pan?" Bo thought his comment was hilarious. Red thought it was equally amusing. I sat in the back of the car with Jess and we discussed all things baby. I hoped that she would deliver before I left to go back to the city.

"You guys going to Unc's tonight? I'm bartending and I think you'll have a welcoming committee there" I looked at Bo and he nodded for both of us.

We made it to Mom's house and she and Dad were sitting on the porch waiting for us. I could picture Bo and I like that in 30 years, but I didn't know if he could ever get away from the city. We could always opt for a bigger place with a balcony.

"My baby girl!" Dad scooped me up when I was barely out of the car. It was nice to have such a warm embrace. I was starting to get really excited for the weekend ahead of us.

Bo put our belongings in my room, which my mother kept referring to the guest room even though it was my room and still decorated the same as it was 10 years ago.

I followed him into the room, and found Bo wearing my beauty sash and tiara. "Bo, you look so beautiful." I tried to hold in my laughter knowing that it just encouraged him to keep going.

He was doing his best beauty queen wave when Red came into the room.

"What are you doing Homo?" Bo chased after him, causing my entire family to erupt into hysterics. It was like Bo had been born into this family. I couldn't remember it being this way on our last visit, but I guess our situation was hardly the same then anyway.

Mom made us dinner, spaghetti which was a household favorite.

"I haven't had a home cooked meal in months." Bo looked right at me.

"Izabella! I taught you better than that!"

"For the love mom he is pulling your chain. Of course, I cook for him, and rub his feet, and his back and⋯."

"Alright. Alright I'm going to be sick." Red held his hands up in the air in surrender.

Everyone began getting ready to go out, while I helped my mom clean up in the kitchen. She

pulled me in for a hug and whispered in my ear "Does he know yet?"
I assumed that she meant Jer and about the wedding. "I'm not sure I haven't talked to him since right before."
"I mean Bo. Does he know that you're pregnant?"
I looked at her in complete shock. "How did you?"
She smiled with satisfaction. "Your boobs have never been that big in your whole life. So when are you going to tell him?" I told her that I was waiting for the right time, the perfect moment, and looking for the best idea. "Izabella, the perfect time anytime that you tell him. That man is completely infatuated with you, he will be on cloud 9 no matter the place, the time or the way that you decide to tell him."
I nodded in agreement; I don't know why I had been racking my brain this whole time. We finished cleaning and then all piled into the car to go to Unc's with the exception of Jess who decided to go to bed early, and not be exposed to the smoke-filled bar at 9 months pregnant. "It's bad enough that I get his secondhand stench when he crawls into bed at 4 am."
I saw red bend down and kiss her belly, then come up to kiss her cheek. "Take care of my girl, and you call me if you need anything." It seemed like there was a magnetic force between them, and it took everything in him to pull away. "It's like this every time he leaves her." Mom looked at me and smiled.
It warmed my heart and I nodded back to her mirroring our immense pride in him. The drive to the bar was a short one. We all piled out of the car, and when I saw the number of cars there I knew that it was more than just a regular night out to catch up.
We walked in and a huge congratulations banner was hung above the bar. The ceiling was filled with balloons wall to wall. I was so overwhelmed and I looked over to Bo and saw that we shared the emotion.

He pulled me into him and then dipped me and kissed me, in front of everyone. The crowd erupted in cheer. It was like we were local celebrities.

Red came up with two glasses of champagne and we made our way to the bar. He jumped on the bar and pulled out a piece of paper. Enough to send me over the edge in tears and he hadn't even spoken a word.

"First of all, I want to thank you all for coming! We all know that Iz isn't the easiest to get along with, but somehow this fool has managed to follow her around for 7 years. Bo, thanks for making my big sister manageable to be around. Iz, I don't say it often enough but we all know Bo is one lucky son of a bitch. I wish you both the best. All my love." He held up his beer and everyone hollered again.

Two hours into the night, you would have thought that this was Bo's hometown. He had a group around him all night long, mostly of girls but I still wasn't the slightest bit jealous. I knew that they could never offer him the things that I could, or the unbreakable bond that we had.

I saw him glance up and head my way, and I got butterflies in my stomach. It was like a movie the way he parted through the crowd to find me, to be near me.

Once he reached me he whispered in my ear "I missed you."

Just those words brought tears to my eyes again, I realized that the hormones were probably taking over my brain.

"Is everything ok?" He pulled away from me looking concerned. "Yes. I'm just really happy."

"Hey I want to take you somewhere, you think we can sneak out of here?"

I pointed to the back door, and we started walking towards the water. I could hear the waves crashing on the shore before I could see it. It made my pulse quicken with excitement, and the smell filled my soul.

We made it to the beach without saying a word to one another. Bo walked me under the pier and pressed my back against the cool wood. "I just had to have you to myself for just a few minutes. I'm not used to sharing you." He pulled me into a kiss and everything was heightened. I could smell his cologne which seemed like heaven, I could feel his tongue slowly enter my mouth and his hand moving up and down my side.

"We can go back now, I just needed one kiss." He smiled and pulled my behind him back to the bar. When we snuck back in through the kitchen Red caught us. "You're assholes! I've got shots lined up for you."

I nervously pushed through the crowd behind Bo. He threw back the first shot and looked over at me. I held the glass in my hand, trying to think of a way out of the shot. Problem is it was tequila, and he knew I loved it.

"I ummm… I don't want to be hung over for tomorrow." He took another shot. "One shot won't hurt you, we both know you're a pro Bells." I shook my head, but put the glass down.

"No. No. No." He looked over at the words and me got louder and louder. My stomach felt sick, all attention was now on us. I nodded again. He pulled me in and picked me off of the ground. "I'm going to be a Dad?" I nodded again, unable to verbalize any of it.

Bo started crying, in a bar filled wall to wall of people. Something I never thought I would witness. He turned toward the crowd. "I'm going to be a Dad!" It was in that moment that I saw Jer enter the bar.

My first instinct was to run to him, but I wanted this moment with Bo to be perfect. I looked up again and he was gone. I knew where he would be, but I also knew that I wouldn't be going there.

The rest of the night was quite the celebration. Even my Mom was drinking, and she was telling all of my forbidden embarrassing stories, which included the time that I was attacked by the beater in fifth grade while making pancakes. My Dad kept his arm around Bo the whole night as if he was a trophy. I was glad that I married someone that my Dad was proud of; he would be the toughest critic. It wasn't until a week after my wedding that I even found out that Bo asked my Dad for his permission before he asked me to marry him.

Not that my father had a choice, because we both knew that I was going to marry him regardless. I was ready to go home, and I knew that I was the only sober one so I offered them all a ride, which they loudly, but politely declined.

"Alright you guys. Walk home safely then!" I would have to set my alarm for about an hour after the bar closed just to catch a glimpse of them all stumbling in.

My headlights hit the porch and my heart stopped. I saw a head covered by an oversized USMC hoodie. I sat in the car for two minutes before getting out. I even contemplated going back to the bar. I realized though, that this was an issue that I was going to have to address at one point in time. I couldn't ignore the red envelopes any longer.

I got out of the car and saw him look up with his face covered in tears. Jer was stronger than this. I ran to him and put my arms around him. "It's ok Jer."
" I would have given anything, I mean anything for that to be me and you there tonight."

I didn't know what to say so I didn't say anything at all. "You didn't read my letters did you?" I shook my head. For all I knew they could have been empty.

"I figured you wouldn't. I still know you the best." He said it with conviction. I even wondered if he was being passive aggressive by writing them to me. "Jer, it's not a competition." I heard full-blown weeping; I pulled his face to look at me. "What happened to you?" He was broken. "Nothing, it just breaks my heart that you are with him. It should have been me."

"Bullshit. Jer I know you better than anyone else too. Tell me what is going on."

"You should have read your letters, if you had you wouldn't be here comforting me." Now I was wishing I had read those letters. What could be so horrible that I wouldn't want to comfort my oldest friend when he is in so much pain.

"Jer, I need you to tell me now or to leave. We can't do this and you know it."

"Are you happy with him? Are you sure that he is the one for you?" I nodded.

"I have never been more sure of anything in my life. I wish it could have been you Jer. That was my childhood dream, but we can't just force our heart to want something because it seems like a fairy tale. Because on paper it looks good. In fact, I really owe you a thank you, and it might hurt now but you need to hear it. You led me to him. You made him become the man that stole my heart. I'm not it for you either. You'll know that once you find the woman for you."

He looked at me through glassy eyes "Iz. It was my baby." I had just been sucker punched. "What do you mean Jer!" My mind was going at record speed. "I didn't know it was mine until she lost it. I did love her. I was going to be a Dad. I did sleep with her that night, but it was out of pain, and guilt that I wasn't there for her when I should have been." His voice was breaking, and I felt like my heart was breaking all over again.

I was happy with Bo, and I knew that I couldn't be happier with anyone else but I felt a new form of betrayal. This changed my entire perspective of Jer, it was like I was staring at a stranger. The part of me that wanted to comfort my best friend disappeared. I had begun to question the validity of our friendship at all.

"I'm sorry for your loss Jer." I got up and headed towards the door to the house. I looked back and saw the shell of Jer sitting on my porch. I turned the light off and walked into the house.

Jess came and put her arms around me. "I heard the whole thing. I'm really sorry." I was so sick of the word sorry. It didn't take away the pain I felt, it didn't take away the fact that I let myself believe someone I trusted for far too long. I needed peace, and sorry wouldn't give me that. I needed to disconnect myself completely from Jer. He started banging on the door and I could hear the mumbling,

"I'm so fucking sorry Iz. I'm so sorry." There it is again. The thing is I wasn't sure what he was sorry for.

I reluctantly opened the door. "Jer. I cannot hear you say I am sorry one more time. I need you to leave." I saw Bo walking up behind Jer.

"What's going on here?" I could tell he was buzzed and genuinely confused.
Jer looked over at him. "Just saying my last goodbye is all." He turned and walked away. Relief that finally Bo was home overcoming the pain inside me.

He pulled me into him. His scent comforted me, and I wished I didn't ever have to pull away from him. "I thought you were staying longer." I looked up into his ice blue eyes.

"I missed you." That was all I needed to hear from him. That was the best description of what I had with him. I knew that no matter where life would take us, if we weren't together I would always miss him, and that's why Bo was the one for me.

Bo asked me no questions about what had happened between Jer and I. That night I wasn't ready to talk about it. The only thing I wanted to do was be with Bo, and I was over and over again that night. We had so much to be happy for, so much to celebrate.

Just as he was falling asleep he whispered, "I always knew you would be the mother of my child." I pulled his arms tightly around me and fell to sleep.

Chapter Forty-Three

I was in the middle of a dream when I felt a heavy weight on top of me. I woke up to see Ella with her arms wrapped around me. "I missed you Mama." Bo was behind her in the doorway drinking his coffee. I sat up and my happiness reflected on Bo's face.

"Hey you! I've missed you so much." I looked around for a box in the room. I pointed to the stuffed animals and Bo dug through them finally finding the present. He handed it to me and nodded in approval.

"Hey Ella girl, your Daddy and I want you to open this."

"Is it a dress for the party tonight?" I shook my head.

She unwrapped the gift faster than a kid on Christmas Morning. Without saying a word, I saw Ella beam with a new ray of happiness!

"Its····.Its just what I always wanted." She held the shirt up to her that read Big Sister. "Is it real? Am I really going to be a big sister?"

Bo found his way to the bed. "It's a real baby girl. It's real." We all sat on my childhood bed with Bo's arms wrapped around us. As a little girl I sat in this very bed spending so many nights dreaming for this.

Epilogue:

Bo

I couldn't believe that Bella was already six months pregnant. I sat on the couch staring at her dancing around in the kitchen while making dinner. She was a vision, my vision. I looked at her and gently place her hand on her stomach as she looked over at me.

"He's moving! He must like this song." I laughed at the Justin Bieber song blaring through our home.

"I doubt that, he's probably trying to get your attention to turn it off."

"Be nice Bo." She gave me a stern look that no one would believe she was capable of. "I'm going to get in the shower, keep an eye on the chicken." She leaned in and kissed my forehead and it felt like heaven.

I made my way into the kitchen and stared at all the letters in a pile on the counter. It tore me up that she hadn't opened them, mostly because I was dying to know what the asshole had to say for himself.

I picked up the stack of envelopes and guessed there had to be at least twenty. I picked one from the middle and ran my finger over the seam. My conscience told me no, but curiosity finally won me over.

I ripped the envelope and looked up to be sure she didn't hear it, although realistically it probably didn't even make a sound.

I unfolded the letter and seeing his handwriting alone had my blood boiling.

Dear Iz,

I can't take one more second of not being able to talk to you. I hate the way we left things, and I need to know that you told Bo the truth.

That's it. That's all I could handle on an empty stomach. I heard my girl coming around the corner so I shoved the letter back in the pile. *What is the truth?* She ran up to me as if she hadn't seen me in ages and I placed my hand on her stomach. "Is he still moving?" She nodded her head, but what I really wanted to ask was *"Is he mine?"*